I0567073

Just Fall

By Annica Rossi

Copyright

Just Fall

By Annica Rossi

Kindle Edition

Copyright © Annica Rossi 2013

Published By Annica Rossi, LLC 2013

All rights reserved. No part of this publication can be reproduced, scanned or

distributed in any printed or electronic form without the author's permission

with the exception of short quotes used in book reviews.

This is a work of fiction, and any names, characters, places, and incidents are

the product of the author's imagination or are used fictitiously. Any resemblance

to actual persons, living or dead, events, or locales Is entirely coincidental.

The publisher does not have any control over and does not assume any

responsibility for author or third-party websites or their content.

Acknowledgements

A special heartfelt thank you goes out to all my friends and family who never stop believing in me no matter how outrageous my ideas may seem and to my beta readers, whose time and dedication have helped make this book possible.

Finally, THANK YOU to each and every person who has purchased and/or read my book. I hope you enjoy my work! As long as you're out there, I will continue to give you my very best.

Prologue

"One of my favorite things about Lake Michigan is that it seems to go on forever like the ocean, and visitors who see it for the first time are often amazed when they realize they can't see the other side."

"As humans it's our nature to want to see everything, and I'm no exception. Not knowing what's in store is a hard pill to swallow, especially when it seems like everything's falling apart. This lake reminds me that sometimes I'm better off not seeing so far ahead. Sometimes I need to be patient and appreciate each little part as it's revealed, otherwise I might miss all there is to discover along the way." – Lauren St. John

Contents

One

A MOMENT IN TIME

Looking around the crowded tavern I realize "this is it." This is what I've been waiting for. The countless caffeine fueled nights I'd spent pacing the floor, pouring over financials, plotting my battle plan to get The Grandview Inn whole again, looks like they're finally paying off. And, not a moment too soon.

With every room booked for the weekend, people were crowded into the rustic wood booths and tables in intimate groups, their laughter rising above the clatter of dishes and the exhilarating beat of live music resonating from the stage. It was still early for a Friday night, but even the dance floor was packed with countless pairs of cowboy boots, stilettos and summer sandals moving in and out of the shadowy stage lights. Mouthwatering smells from the grill combined with alcohol, suntan lotion and fresh lake air created an intoxicating cocktail inviting visitors to leave their troubles at the door. My heart swelled with pride as I took in the scene. The Grand was alive and buzzing with activity. You could almost feel her heartbeat. Filled to capacity for the first time in months, it was definitely a good sign things were finally turning around.

"Hey, Lo, can you grab some shot glasses from the back?" Steve shouted over the roar of the crowd as he worked on installing a keg.

"Yeah! Need anything else?" I smiled at him appreciatively as I wished I had ten more Steves on a night like this.

"Straws and cocktail napkins. That should do it."

I nodded in acknowledgement as I made my way to the back room. It had been a while since I worked the bar, but it always felt familiar, just like riding a bicycle. Tonight it was more like riding a bicycle downhill with the wind whipping through my hair. I loved it.

As I scanned the shelves for the supplies, I caught a glimpse of the lines drawn in permanent black marker on the door casing. Every time I saw those lines, I felt happy and sad at the same time. Sounds crazy I know, but it's like the feeling that comes from looking at a photograph from a time when everything was perfect and realizing you can never go back.

Those lines looked faded and forgotten now, but they'll always be my photograph. My dad used to measure my height right here against this door. It was our tradition until I was a teenager, and I still see him standing here like it was yesterday, marker in hand smiling from ear-to-ear. Lost in thought, I traced my finger over the worn numbers.

Every memory of my childhood lives in these walls. My mom and dad bought this place before I was born. The Grandview Inn was the only home I'd ever known. A smile tugged at my lips as I looked from my dad's scribbled numbers to the boxes in my hands.

I could hear his voice in my head. Every time he caught me doing a "staff job" he would say the same thing, "Lo, we have people for that." He tried to sound stern, but he would laugh with a twinkle of pride in his eyes. He never spoiled me, he just wanted me to "work smarter not harder." He sent me off to Michigan State University just to make sure of it. Dad never went to college himself, and he and mom did every job around here in the early years. It's hard to believe they turned a shabby run-down motel into the graceful gem that so many people affectionately referred to as "The Grand."

It was the perfect name for his masterpiece, and he left traces of his heart and soul everywhere. He may have called me his "Golden Girl," but she was his first love, even above mom at times. When I got older I understood why. Everything about her was beautiful, from her detailed white cornices to her high peaked rooftops. She towered over the other buildings, and from a distance she looked like she was coming right out of the mountainous hillside. She had wide white porches that seemed to wrap around for miles. Balconies overlooked the shore from the rear rooms, while dormers crowned the lines of large windows in the front, and in the backyard her curves followed the shoreline of Lake Michigan. But even better than her stunning beauty was the feeling she gave you when you're here. It was magical.

The door opened and music poured into the stockroom followed by Steve's face peeking through the crack.

"Sorry! I was just coming out." I tried to sound confident, but the look on my face must have given me away.

With a quick apology, Steve ducked out of the room. *Now's not the time for a stroll down memory lane, Lo.* Drawing a deep breath, I walked back into the bar.

Steve grabbed the boxes from me and flashed a contagious smile. "Hey, do you hear that?"

I smiled back with wide eyes and nodded my head. My insides felt warm and fuzzy. I knew exactly what he meant. The energy and excitement in the air felt like Christmas morning when The Grand was firing on all cylinders, and tonight was just like old times - a full house.

"Looks like this band can really draw a crowd, huh?"

"I'll say," he replied giving me a fist bump as he walked past.

It was going to be a long night, and I needed to change my clothes. I was still in my office attire and my feet were already killing me. I bent down next to Steve grabbing the napkins. "We could use at least two more bartenders in here tonight."

"Yes, we could, but who knew? This is the busiest we've been in a long time."

"I know it's fucking amazing!" I couldn't stop gushing. "Think you could spare me for a minute while I run upstairs and change?"

"No worries. Shawn and Matt are on their way. Besides, with you dressed like that our guests won't know whether to order a drink or make a reservation."

Laughing loudly, I could feel the tension in my shoulders unwinding, and I gave myself permission to relax a bit. As much as I wanted to believe the entire summer would be this good, I knew I still had a lot of work ahead of me, even so, I decided to enjoy this night while it lasted.

"And that's why I pay you the big bucks, Steve, always one step ahead of me," I shot back.

The band announced a fifteen minute intermission, and the dance floor began to clear. My collar was sticking to the back of my neck from working behind the bar for the last two hours, and I was a hot mess. I was looking forward to a quick shower and some fresh clothes before coming back down to help out and mingle with the guests.

I scanned the room waiving at a few familiar faces as I planned my exit. Needing some fresh air, I headed for the patio door. Outside, the sound of waves crashing on the beach greeted me, and the light breeze made my clothes feel damp against my skin. I had just reached the staircase when I heard someone call out my name.

"Lauren! Lo, over here, dear!"

I looked up at the door to my suite. *Damn it!* I was so close, but I knew I had to turn around. I would recognize Mary Blackwell's voice anywhere.

The Blackwell family had been staying at The Grandview for years. I played with their daughter Sarah every summer vacation from the time we were four until we went off to college, and we still kept in touch, mostly through emails and the occasional phone call. But Mary? She was like a second mother to me, not to mention one of my most loyal customers. I always looked forward to seeing her, even at a time like this.

I turned around with a warm smile and greeted the woman whose presence always put me at ease. "Mary! I'm so happy to see you!"

"Nonsense! Come here you," she beamed as she pushed her chair back and held her arms out to me.

The familiar smell of Chanel No. 5 wafted all around me as I squeezed her, and when her lips smacked loudly against my cheek, I knew she was leaving her signature red lipstick marks behind, but I didn't mind. Her loving embrace temporarily made me forget how terrible I looked. Besides, Mary wasn't uptight about appearances. She came from old money, but aside from my own mother she was the most down-to-earth, genuine woman I'd ever met.

She held me at arm's length for examination. "You're beautiful as ever, Lo, but you look a little skinny. Have you been taking care of yourself? By the looks of this place, you've probably been working way too hard, haven't you?"

"No, I'm fine, Mary. Even better now that you're here." I looked at the table and spotted her Merlot along with two empty rocks glasses. "Where's Tom?" He must be nearby. Mary has never come to The Grand without her husband of 40 years.

"Oh, he's here, honey. He went up to get us a couple more drinks. It's so busy here tonight."

"I know! I'm sorry. This crowd was totally unexpected. We have more staff coming in as we speak."

"It's fine, dear. Hell, we'd come back here even if we had to make our own drinks!"

She always made me laugh. "I love you, Mary!" I hugged her again.

"Are you going to be out here a while? I need to go upstairs and change out of this suit, but I'd love to join you when I'm done." As I spoke, Mary was motioning to someone over my shoulder.

"That sounds lovely, dear. I can't wait to spend the evening with you, but just a minute there's someone I want you to see first."

I was immediately filled with dread at the prospect of greeting her guest in my disheveled condition, but I knew Mary Blackwell too well. Once she had her mind set on something she wouldn't take no for an answer, so I smoothed my hands down the sides of my skirt and prepared to greet one of Tom's business partners or one of the many couples they'd vacationed with after their kids left home.

As soon as I turned around, I felt the color drain from my face, and my smile quickly faded. I wanted to crawl under the nearest table, but my feet felt like they were cemented in place, and I had to remind myself to breathe. Just a few feet away stood the most intriguingly gorgeous, tall, blonde and dangerously fuckable man I had ever laid eyes on. His perfect white teeth and deep dimples were slowly revealed as an inviting smile spread across his lips, and I noticed immediately the way his mouth curled at the corners just a little. I swore I felt testosterone radiating from his very presence as even the air seemed to thicken, instantly impregnated with seduction and mischief.

And his hair! He had bedroom hair. I don't mean in the bedhead kind of way. I mean in the "I could bang any bitch in this room and leave her begging for more" kind of way. When his emerald green eyes locked on mine, I was mesmerized. The blood that had obviously drained from my face headed south to my stomach and beyond causing my thighs to tighten as an intense warmth swirled through my lower regions. *What the hell?*

I quickly closed my mouth and tried desperately to regain my composure, even as my disobedient eyes continued to greedily devour every last inch of him. They noticed how the breeze pressed his white, V-neck, T-shirt tightly against his body, causing it to cling to every sculpted line of his rock-hard six-pack before traveling downward to evaluate the possibility that the rest of him could be as equally impressive. *Get a fucking grip, Lo!*

I'm not normally attracted to bad boys, and he was the perfect specimen, but there was an air of confidence about him that came from more than just his stunning good looks, and it beckoned me to investigate. He was picture perfect in every way…but as you know looks can be deceiving.

As I recovered from my momentary brain lapse vague memories began to surface in the back of my mind. *I couldn't put my finger on it, but there was something very familiar about those dimples...*

Mary's voice jarred me from my daydream. "Parker, you remember Lauren St. John, don't you? Lo, do you remember my nephew, Parker Blackwell?"

Seriously? Just fucking shoot me now. How could I forget?

We stood there bewildered as we shook hands. I couldn't help but notice how mine fit entirely inside of his, and how even as I let go he held on for just a few seconds longer. Then suddenly, as if we were looking in the mirror his hand went to his cheek at the same time as mine to wipe the red lipstick marks away. We both smiled, and his eyes seemed to penetrate the invisible shield I was trying to put up between us. It was almost like he was reading my thoughts when his expression turned darker and his tongue slowly dragged across his bottom lip. *Predatory.* Our smiles quickly faded, and I wondered briefly if he had picked up on the effect he had on me.

"You, Sarah and Parker were like The Three Musketeers all those summers! It seems like just yesterday!" Mary continued, "I couldn't wait to see you two together again. I wish Sarah were here. She'd be sad to know she missed this reunion."

Reunion? Aside from the unexpected, albeit intense fireworks just now, this felt more like a nightmare than a reunion! The sudden flood of emotions caught me off guard. Seeing him again hurt more than I cared to admit.

Thankfully, Tom broke the tension. "Lo, come here and hug me! You get more and more beautiful each summer."

"Thanks, Tom." I felt my cheeks blush as he lifted me off my feet in one of his famous bear hugs.

Mary finally approached the elephant in the room. "We're so sorry about your dad."

I tried to swallow the lump that instantly formed in my throat. "Yes, thank you. And thank you for the thoughtful letter and flowers, too."

"We meant what we said, Lo." Mary's voice was soft and full of motherly concern. "Tom and I will always be here for you."

They must have heard that Evelyn inherited a share of The Grand, and I knew they felt responsible. They brought her here the summer after my mom died, and at the time she was married to one of Tom's partners in the investment firm—I think he was husband number three, but that didn't stop her from going after my dad. Tom and Mary had no way of knowing what a mess this would turn out to be. I knew they would never do anything to hurt me, and I didn't blame them for it.

I lied, "Everything's fine really."

Just then I felt Parker's eyes on me. *Just what I need- for him to see a sign of weakness!* "Well, I'm going to go change my clothes. I'll be back to join you in a bit." I needed to get out of there quick. I started walking toward the staircase without giving Mary a chance to throw up another road block, but halfway up I heard her voice calling over my shoulder.

"Hurry back, Lo. We'll be right here waiting for you."

Two

ROOM WITH A VIEW

At twenty-five-years-old I was living a life most men only dreamed about. My career as a professional poker player took me to faraway places and afforded me exquisite food and exotic women. I've tried everything once, some things hundreds of times, but never a woman-no matter how hot she was or how good between the sheets, or in the hot tub, or on the balcony…you get the idea. One night stands were my cardinal rule.

I know. I know. You're thinking I'm some kind of despicable pig who uses women then carelessly tosses them out like yesterday's newspaper, but believe me, the type of women I choose already know the score. Whether they like it fast and rough or slow and sensual, when it's over, it's over. No future plans, no late night phone calls, no drama, no bullshit. Judge me if you will, but this lifestyle was working pretty well for me. Little did I know that one phone call was about to change everything…

Neon light spilled through the windows illuminating the pair of perfectly shaped breasts bouncing inches from my face. The sounds and smells of raw sex permeated the air in the master bedroom of my penthouse suite as I watched Lexi's face contort in pleasure welcoming each thrust of my rock hard cock. Lost in the sensation as she rode me hard, gripping me expertly in her slippery warmth, I barely noticed Ashley's nipple brushing against my cheek as the mattress jerked violently beneath us. I turned and caught the hard little peak between my teeth making her moan and squirm, and a smile stretched across my lips.

I was nursing a badly bruised ego, after an unexpected loss at my last tournament, and my appetite for sex was at an unprecedented high, even for me. The three of us had been going at it for hours, and it seemed even these two insatiable beauties couldn't wear me out. I became painfully aware that things would need to get a lot more interesting for me to find my release tonight.

Lexi's high pitched screams were quickly followed by her hot cunt contracting wildly around me. I grabbed her hips and thrust faster as she screamed, begging me to fuck her harder before her body finally went rigid, and she collapsed against my chest. She barely recovered before Ashley was trying to claim her position, but I had something else in mind. I freed myself gently from the weight of their bodies, noticing the disappointed pout on Ashley's face, and ordered her to kneel down in front of me and straddle Lexi's face in a sixty-nine position-the ultimate visual stimulation. I watched over Ashley's shoulder, fervently stroking my cock as they pleasured each other. When the licking and moaning reached a fever pitch, I slammed relentlessly into the hot waiting pussy in front of me, not slowing down until it milked the last drops of cum from my trembling body.

Exhausted, I dropped onto the nearest pillow and collapsed, but oddly enough, sleep didn't come as easily as I'd hoped. Instead my mind was racing, trying to understand why lately the sex wasn't quite as fulfilling as it was in the past. I mean the women were hot as hell, and the pleasure was mind-blowing, but it seemed like something was missing, like each time I needed a little more to feel as good as I did the time before. Even after I was completely spent, I still wasn't satisfied. It didn't make sense, and if I let myself get too hung up on it, something like this could really fuck with my head.

I told myself it was *just temporary.* Probably the result of letting that rookie whip my ass at the table last week, and I was already working hard to make sure that didn't happen again. Thanks to modern technology, I spent the last two days studying the footage from the final tables. I learned his tells, and realized my own fatal mistakes. The next tournament would be in Vegas, my turf, and I would be ready for him.

My eyes blinked open slowly, trying to adjust to the sunlight pouring through the windows overlooking the Vegas strip, and I could hear the faint sound of my phone ringing from somewhere in the room. Any other time it would take a lot more than a phone call to pry me from the arms of two lovely naked bodies like these, but I had a strange feeling this could be important, so I climbed carefully out of bed to find out.

"Parker! You sound tired. I hope I didn't wake you, dear. What time zone are you in?"

I'd never felt dirtier than I did standing there, listening to the sound of Aunt Mary's sweet voice as my eyes watched the scene taking place in the middle of my bed. I took one last peek at Lexi's attempt to wake Ashley using only her tongue before I shut the door behind me and reluctantly walked into the other room. How could something be so wrong and so right at the same time?

"Hi, Aunt Mary! What a surprise!" *If she only knew.* "You're fine. I'm in Vegas for two weeks, so I've been up for a while now." *Nearly all night as a matter-of-fact.*

"Oh, good, well I'm glad you're stateside. Uncle Tom and I want you to come north with us for the weekend to visit The Grandview Inn. Our chauffeur had to leave for a family emergency, and your uncle doesn't like to drive that far alone anymore. I know this probably sounds silly. Surely, we could hire another driver temporarily, but you know, I couldn't help but think of all the good memories we made at The Grand over the years. Oh, Parker, it would mean so much to us if you could come."

Fuck! Fuck, fuck, fuck, fuck!

Remember when I said my instincts told me to answer the phone? Until now I'd considered them finely tuned, sharpened even, from my experience at the poker table, but in this case they'd failed me miserably. I mean The Grandview Inn? Really? That was the last place on Earth I wanted to go. Remember my cardinal rule? Yeah, well that's where it all began.

How can I get out of this? Think, think...

"Listen, Aunt Mary, as much as I'd like to..." That was as far as I got. The woman had a way with words, and I had a hard time saying no to her. By the end of the conversation it was settled. I was going to Michigan.

As I stood there naked, the phone still in my hand, I heard noises coming from my bedroom. *I should be in the middle of that right now.* Before that phone call I would've been, before my mind went back to The Grand and all the memories of her started flooding my brain.

She was the first girl I ever loved. Hell, she was the only girl I ever loved. I could still picture her bright hazel eyes with ribbons of orange scattered through them. I've never seen eyes like hers before. They would glare at me with sexy determination over something I said or did, and sometimes I would do things on purpose just to see her look at me that way. She could always see right through me. She was beautiful, smart, funny and incredibly complicated. *Wonder what she's like now?*

I was eighteen the last time I saw her. If she only knew how she ruled my world back then, how many nights I spent lying awake thinking about her, or how many times I challenged her just to see her fiery spirit come to life. Not to mention how many hours I spent with dirty magazines trying to relieve my pent up and painfully unfulfilled desire for her.

But like I said, I was only eighteen. I didn't know how to deal with what she did to me. So instead I provoked her, teased her and tormented her until she pretty much hated my guts. It was my defense mechanism, my survival instinct I guess you could say. Not the best strategy I'll admit, but the only one I could think of at the time.

Sometimes it was worth it. I mean, seeing her so frustrated, so confident. Fuck! It was a turn-on. She would get this look on her face, and I didn't know whether she wanted to punch me or rip my clothes off and fulfill all my secret fantasies. I was willing to take either. Anything to put me out of my misery. I've never met another woman like her. She stood up to me, challenged me right back, and sometimes she won. Other times I let her win.

Like the time I bet I could swim to shore faster than her. We dove off the boat at the same time, and when I surfaced her bikini top was floating on the water. She was so determined to beat me she didn't even notice she'd lost it.

That's when I got the brilliant idea to let her get ahead. I'll never forget the sight of her standing on the beach with her hands on her hips waiting for me. Her chest was heaving with every breath. Strands of her long blonde hair stuck to her face and dripped down her tan body. Her nipples were fully extended from the cold water and adrenaline. She had me so worked up I had to stay in the water for an hour waiting for my hard-on to go down.

Seven years later, the thought of her had the same effect on me, but only now it was mixed with regret. Everything changed that summer her mom got sick, and I decided I would never see her again. Maybe I was a coward, or I was just too young and immature to realize what she meant to me, but knowing that her mom was dying, knowing there wasn't a damn thing I could do to save her from the pain, was more than I could take. So instead of facing her, I didn't go to Michigan. In fact, I never went back, and I convinced myself she was better off without me.

The regret still gets to me from time to time, but until now I'd managed to block it out, justify it even, and my lifestyle made it easy, but facing her meant facing my biggest fear, the one thing that could take a man down in one fatal blow. The "L" word.

You see, my childhood left no doubt that there was no such thing as happily ever after. Well, maybe in some rare instances like Uncle Tom and Aunt Mary, but they were one in a million. I realized at a very young age that there was a difference between love and sex, and I when I got older I decided I could easily have one without the other. This imaginary, yet very real, line I drew was my safety zone, and I stayed well within the boundaries. I occupied myself with things that were fast and furious like gambling, travel, women, and cars. I had no complaints, especially when it came to women. They were in endless supply, and my bed was never empty unless I was focused on a tournament.

And the sex. My intense need for sex concerned me at times. Could I ever be monogamous? Would I be satisfied? My sexual appetite was unconventional at best and not just in frequency. I craved the variety that seemed to accompany my lifestyle, so I decided a long time ago that I was better off alone, and nothing's going to change that, not even Lauren St. John. I'm overanalyzing I know, but much like poker, there were too many unknown variables in this equation, and I had to be careful.

One thing's for sure, every woman I've been with only confirmed what I already knew from the moment I met her. She was the real deal. The total package. She didn't care about my looks, my last name or even my money. She wouldn't take my shit or anyone else's. It was hard to believe that in just two short days I would see her again. It scared the hell out of me.

Maybe she was happily married to Mr. Safe and Responsible. Hell, maybe she even had a couple kids by now. But what if she wasn't? Would it even matter?

The best I could hope for was that she'd forgive and forget. And maybe, just maybe, she'd want to go a few rounds in bed to make up for old times. Fuck! Just thinking about giving Lo a little tour of my world had my cock raging. Would she give me a run for my money or just run away disgusted? I was about to find out, and either way I knew I was in for one hell of a ride. But for now she was 2,000 miles away, and I had two hot women right in the other room who were more than happy to share...

Three

OPPOSITES COLLIDE

My body was still trembling when I reached the safety of my suite. I slammed the door and immediately began pacing like a caged animal. *What was he doing here? And what the hell just happened out there?*

The Parker Blackwell I remembered was the most annoying, frustrating, immature boy I'd ever met, and he always, I mean always had to win. He challenged me at everything, and my entire summers were spent competing with him.

I grabbed my phone and tried to call my best friend, Nina. She knew our history, and she was the only person who would understand what I was going through right now. Straight to voicemail. *Shit!*

This may seem like an outrageous reaction coming from a twenty-four-year-old woman, but if you only knew the torture I endured you would understand. He got under my skin in every way, and although I never admitted it to anyone, I secretly loved him and hated him all at the same time. He was exhausting, sexy and maddening, and I daydreamed about him constantly. He was the reason I practiced kissing my pillow at night, and in the spring I would count the days until he arrived to begin our confusing and frustrating game all over again. Sometimes I thought that he might like me, too. I often caught him staring at me, and that time we kissed he made an attempt at second base, but I never really knew for sure. Everything was just a game to Parker.

I still couldn't believe he was here. He was all grown up now and very easy on the eyes, very, very easy, I might add. Even so, I had a feeling that underneath all that sexy swagger he was the same competitive annoying asshole. I couldn't imagine him any other way.

And if that wasn't bad enough, the last time I saw him was the summer my mom found out she had breast cancer. Talk about bad memories. When he didn't return the following year, I had a ton of mixed emotions that I couldn't explain. I decided I hated him, and convinced myself I was relieved. As much as I wanted to, I never even asked Sarah where he was.

Now you know where he is, Lo! He's downstairs on your patio looking like a fucking model off the cover of GQ. He's sitting right down there with his fuck-me hair, sculpted body and that smile that could charm the pants off Mother Theresa. That's where he is!

It didn't matter that we were all grown up now. The sight of him still had me torn between wanting to kiss him and wanting to punch him in the face.

I tried dialing again. *Where the hell was Nina?* She was the only one who could talk me through this. I threw the phone on the bed in frustration at the sound of her voicemail message again.

Panicking, I started to think of a million excuses to avoid seeing him again, each one sounding more ridiculous than the last. After carefully considering everything from a sudden illness to an unforeseen emergency, I realized I had to face him. As much as I wanted to avoid Parker, I missed Mary and Tom, and I looked forward to catching up on all the latest news about Sarah and her new husband. Were they planning to have children soon? Did they find a house yet?

Besides, things were different now. I'm not the same seventeen-year-old girl Parker knew. I had bigger things to worry about now, like how the hell to keep The Grand rockin' like it was tonight, not to mention how to keep Evelyn, my wicked stepmother, from calling to ask why her quarterly profit checks were getting smaller. Ever since my dad died, Evelyn has been my silent partner in The Grand. Lately she hasn't been so silent, and I wanted nothing more than to get her off my back.

I showered in record time, applied some makeup and unpinned my hair letting the blonde waves fall loosely down my back. As I walked to the closet I knew just what I would wear. The strapless coral sundress that showcased the girls nicely was calling my name along with the silver choker and my dangly silver earrings. *Perfect!*

I took one last look at myself and checked my phone for calls from Nina as I slipped into my strappy sandals in front of the mirror. *Do you still want to challenge me Mr. Blackwell? Well bring it on! This girl is all grown up now and won't waste one more second on the likes of you!*

I decided to take the elevator down to the ground floor so I could stop at the bar and check in with Steve. Parker would be expecting me to come back down the stairs, but that my friends would be his first mistake. The element of surprise would give me the advantage.

Back in the tavern I observed Steve working his magic behind the bar. He was entertaining a group of rowdy ladies, who seemed quite happy to wait as he expertly mixed their Cosmos while keeping them flirting and laughing at the same time. I laughed to myself and shook my head when he looked up and nodded at me as if to say "all is well." Then I stopped a waitress to order a round before heading outside. If I remembered correctly Tom was a whiskey guy, and Mary liked her Merlot and as for Parker… After a minute I knew just what to order.

Happy with my thoughtful gesture, I walked smugly toward the patio door, and halted abruptly in my tracks at the scene taking place just outside. Parker was talking to a sexy little blonde. She was so close her D cups were practically under his nose. *Some things never change!*

As I stood there angrily watching the scene unfold, I quickly realized it wasn't him making the advances. Blondie was practically throwing herself at his feet, and by the look on Mary's face, she wasn't impressed. Then Blondie swept her platinum locks over her shoulder exposing the swell of her breasts, and a sexy dimpled grin spread slowly across Parker's face as he took the pen from her hand and wrote something there. *What the hell is going on?*

I had to pause for just a moment. The whole thing caught me off guard, and I wasn't sure what I was feeling. Yeah, I was angry, but why? I had to admit that seeing Parker touch the breast of the blonde bombshell made me angry, and I knew what that implied, but there's no possible way that I was jealous. I convinced myself that disgusted was the right word. Yeah, disgusted, and I didn't know it then, but things were about to get a whole lot worse.

I approached the table just as Blondie made her exit in the opposite direction. For a moment, I wished I knew her name so I could have her barred for the weekend just to save her from the infamous Parker Blackwell. But who was I kidding? Looking around I could easily count at least three more willing victims just waiting for the opportunity to make their way over here to meet Prince Charming. It was futile.

Mary's face lit up when she noticed me. "Sit down, Lo. I want to tell you all about Sarah's new job."

Realizing I would be placed next to Parker, I hesitated, and right on cue he stood and pulled out my chair. *Nice touch, but I see right through your show of kindness, right to your devious little black heart.*

I smiled sweetly looking him square in the eyes, and for an instant he was so close, too close. Alarm bells sounded in my head. *Retreat!* Something dark flashed in his deep green eyes, and before I could process the multitude of sensations this invoked, I was drawn in by his smell, his very presence. My heart leapt in my chest and fluttery winged things swirled in my belly. My God he was pure man! Pure. Man.

I quickly sat down, anxious to feel the stability of the sturdy chair beneath me. That brief face-to-face encounter shook me to the core. For a moment I had forgotten everything, forgotten where I was even, and when I saw the way Mary was studying me I realized I wasn't the only one who noticed. *Was it that obvious?*

I tried to recover, "I ordered us a round. It should be here in a minute, and for the rest of the night drinks are on the house."

"Well, thank you Lo. You didn't have to do that." Tom was beaming.

Just then Tara, our waitress, arrived, "Merlot for the lady, a Grey Goose martini for you Lauren, Bushmills for you sir, and for you Mr. Blackwell, two double shots of Southern Comfort."

I had to stifle a laugh as Parker looked first at Tara and then at me. His eyes narrowed a little and his lips pressed together in a thin line before I saw the little hamster come to life making the wheels turn. *Gotcha!*

"Parker, I never knew you liked Southern Comfort," Tom observed.

"Oh yes," I interjected quickly, "If I remember correctly Parker loves the stuff. To old times," I smirked as I looked at Parker and held up my glass.

The truth is Parker spent one long and torturous night hugging the toilet that last summer. The culprit? Southern

Comfort of course. *That's right. He never saw it coming. Round One goes to Lauren by TKO.*

With that Tom decided to make an official toast. "To friends, family and the future," he said as we clinked our glasses together loudly.

The toast seemed to ease the tension, and I started to relax. I was even enjoying myself in spite of Parker Blackwell's unnerving presence, but I remained hyperaware of his every move. He downed his first double in one gulp, and he didn't waste any time before polishing off the second as he slammed the shot glass down on the table with an audible thump. *Damn! So much for that!* I felt a little defeated until shortly after he excused himself and headed for the men's room. Mary and Tom looked concerned, and I couldn't help but feel a little pang of guilt, maybe even remorse.

I started squirming in my seat fifteen minutes later when he still hadn't returned, and the idea that my impulsive actions might have ruined our friendly gathering had me screaming inside. After all, I hadn't seen the man in seven years, and a lot has changed since then. *Didn't I owe it to Tom and Mary to give him a chance?*

Worried that he may not come back, I interrupted Mary right in the middle of her tale about Sarah's house hunting nightmares, and I could instantly see the disappointment on her face, but when I told her I was going to check on Parker she seemed pleased.

I could be so stupid sometimes. I swore I wouldn't sink to his level, that I wouldn't allow Parker Blackwell to reduce me to childish out-of-control teenager status, yet here I was looking for him, feeling guiltier by the second. I didn't see him anywhere in the bar, so I decided to keep my eye on the men's room. When he didn't come out after a few minutes deep regret settled in. I told myself I didn't care about him anymore, but my behavior said otherwise. *Could I still hate Mr. Tall, Blonde and Dangerously Fuckable?*

Unwilling to give up so easy, I decided to check outside. If I were in his shoes right now I'd need some fresh air. Wherever he was, I had to find him, apologize and try to salvage what was left of this beautiful night. I also had to be careful not to look at him too long or get too close. There was something electric about him, and my body hadn't stopped humming since I laid eyes on him again. *But why?* I couldn't wrap my mind around it. Since he was going to be here all weekend I could only hope for two things-one, that he wouldn't make this apology too hard on me; and two, that my anger could outlast his charm.

As the foyer door swung open, I saw two figures standing in the shadows outside. I could tell by the tall muscly build and white T-shirt that one of them was

Parker. As I walked closer I could clearly see that he wasn't stooped over as I'd imagined. He wasn't sitting down with his head in his hands trying to hold down his dinner either. Nope. *I should've known.*

There he was, his back to the wall, and Blondie was practically climbing down his pants. *And to think I was worried, considering an apology even, while Parker Blackwell was out here getting his motor primed by Miss D Cups! Perfect!*

In hindsight this is where I should have drawn the line, been the bigger person and left well enough alone. But in the heat of the moment I lost my mind at the sight of Blondie getting up close and personal. I guess that's why they call it hindsight.

I instantly saw red, and my impulse to drag her across the parking lot by her hair was overwhelming. I knew I was about to do the unthinkable. I was about to give in to my impulses without measuring the consequences…

I'll never forget the summer I turned fifteen. For a week straight Parker dared me to take my dad's convertible for a drive. He called me a "goody two-shoes," "perfect princess"-anything he could think of to drive me over the edge. Finally, one night, unbeknownst to my dad of course, I decided to prove once and for all that I wasn't the "perfect daddy's girl."

With the stars twinkling above, the radio cranked up, and Parker looking at me like John Travolta looked at Olivia Newton John post bad girl transformation, I was having the time of my life! Right up until the moment those flashing lights appeared in the rear view mirror.

I should have seen it coming, but in the heat of the moment it never occurred to me that my dad might think his car was stolen and call the cops. He never suspected that his "Golden Girl" would have driven off into the night with Danny fucking Zuko. I'll never forget the look on his face when I got out of the back of that cop car.

Hindsight.

Hadn't I learned my lesson by now? Any other time I would say definitely, and unequivocally "yes!" But the dynamic between Parker and me was toxic, addicting—dangerous even.

Trudging straight up to the two of them I let loose. *Let the games begin!*

"There you are, honey! I've been looking all over for you," I feigned shock. "Who the hell is this?"

"Who the hell are you?" Blondie demanded as she stood between us with her hands on her hips.

"I'm his wife. His pregnant wife. Pregnant with twins!" *Okay, maybe that was too much, but I couldn't resist.* "He probably never mentioned me. Did he? Did you?" I looked at Parker expectantly. "My daddy was right about you! You're nothing but a lying cheat!"

And we're off!

"Lo, calm down! Are you off your meds again?" Parker said, playing along and acting genuinely concerned. "Are you?" he demanded. "Oh, no, don't tell me you're on the bottle again? What about the baby?"

"Correction, babi-e-s you asshole!"

"Whoa, whoa, both of you calm down. A pregnant lady shouldn't have to deal with an asshole like you!" Before I realized what was about to happen, Blondie turned to Parker and slapped him hard across the face.

"That was for my cousin in Vegas AND your wife!" she yelled before stomping off toward the parking lot.

Nothing but the sound of our breathing filled the space between us. Nothing but awkward silence, and I didn't fully realize it yet, but it had already started. Parker and Lo. Just like old times.

"What the hell is wrong with you? And to think I actually looked forward to seeing you again. I thought maybe you'd grown up after all this time, but you're still the same psycho uptight bitch you always were! Let's just say I'm sorely disappointed, but not surprised!"

I was gloating momentarily. Blondie was gone, and Parker got a good slap in the face by someone other than me. *Round Two goes to Lauren.*

"Save the bullshit Parker! Why *did* you come here anyway? We're not even friends. I haven't seen or heard from you in seven years, and if I remember correctly YOU were the one who made my life hell! What's wrong? You got bored with the ladies throwing themselves at you in Vegas and decided to come try your luck with me again?

Well, I'm not a little girl anymore, but I can clearly see you're the same little boy."

His eyes grew wide, and then something else. He looked hurt. "I made your life hell? Hah! If it wasn't for me you would've had a stick shoved permanently up your ass - kind of the way you do right now. The only thing I ever did was get you to live a little, Lo! But it looks like that stick has become a permanent fixture!"

With that I smacked him soundly in the same place Blondie did. His cheek instantly turned a brighter shade of red. We stared at each other for a few seconds, listening to the sound of crickets in the flower garden and the hum of the parking lot lights. The tension between us had dialed up ten notches, and adrenaline rushed through me as I realized how fast things had escalated. I waited nervously for his reaction.

Suddenly Parker grabbed me by the wrists and pulled my body roughly against his. The electricity crackled between us and heat seared my skin everywhere his body touched mine. Startled, I looked up trying to read his face.

"I came here to do this," he whispered, and before I could protest, his seductively warm mouth closed over mine.

I tried to pull away from him as pent up anger rolled through me like a thunderstorm. Inside I was screaming, letting him know how much he hurt me when he left all those years ago. I wanted to hate him! I wanted to hate the taste of him, the smell of him so close, but all I could think of was *more.* I wanted more.

The spicy smell of his aftershave mixed with his own unique male scent (pheromones maybe?) were more than I could take. Every part of me responded to him, melted into him. His hands left my wrists and lifted my hair, twisting his fingers through it as his lips and tongue ravaged mine. Liquid heat pooled between my legs, and suddenly I was hyperaware of every detail about him. I was breathing him, inhaling him, tasting him and letting him take what he wanted from me.

For a moment I felt like nothing else in the world mattered. Crushed against his chest, my breasts ached for release. My nipples strained through the thin material of my dress as I imagined him giving them the same skillful attention he was giving my mouth. My hands went to his chest, tugging, pulling at the buttons, tracing a trail over the hard muscles of his stomach. He grabbed my ass and pressed himself roughly into my thigh, and I could feel he wanted me just as much.

When my hands explored lower, lightly skimming the defined v that disappeared just below his jeans, he leaned his head back against the wall. I looked up at him. His white hot expression, his eyelids heavy, the way his lips were slightly parted glistening with saliva from our kiss, urged me to tug his belt open roughly. His chest heaved, and his green eyes filled with lust, awaited my next move. In that brief moment, I realized how much taller he was than me, broader, stronger. He wasn't the same boy I remembered seven years ago. He was a man. A fucking beautiful, passionate man.

The front doors burst open with a flood of laughter sending me spiraling back to earth. Ripping myself from the lewd embrace, I stepped back to adjust my dress and smooth my hair before daring to look.

That's when reality hit me. Here I was a business woman, an engaged business woman at that, standing in front of my inn one button away from fucking a man I haven't laid eyes on in seven years. Five minutes alone with him, and I'd forgotten how bad he hurt me. I'd come completely and entirely undone.

And what about Mary and Tom? They had to be wondering where we went. *What the hell is wrong with you, Lo?*

I knew I couldn't face the two of them. Not like this. They were like parents to me. And then there was Jake. Anxiety flooded through me, and I went into panic mode.

Parker started to speak, and I stopped him as soon as he said my name.

"No, Parker! *This*-whatever *this* is," I waved my hands wildly in the air, "It can never happen again! You haven't even been here one day and I'm acting like a crazy school girl! Not only that, but guess what? I'm engaged, Parker. Yes, that's right. I'm going to marry an incredible man who would never leave me. Who would never drag me out in front of my place of business and practically molest me on the sidewalk!"

I gestured toward the onlookers who are now walking toward their cars still gawking at the Parker and Lauren Show.

His face hardened with every word as if I were landing punches. Direct hits. But his eyes stayed fixed on mine.

"I guess some things never change, do they?"

I slammed my way through the entrance and headed straight to the elevator feeling the weight of his stare on my back until the doors closed behind me.

Four

FRIENDLY ADVICE

I wanted to run. I wanted to put as much distance between me and Parker as I possibly could. For a moment I thought about driving the three hours to where Jake was working for the weekend. If I could just be with him now everything would be okay. I needed him. I needed to tell him what happened.

No, that's the worst thing you could do, Lo! Stay calm and think.

An altercation between Jake and Parker could jeopardize my relationship with The Blackwell Family, and that was a price I wasn't willing to pay. Besides, in the state I'm in I shouldn't be driving anywhere. I only drank one martini, but I was a mess, a total basket case.

Why did he come here? What was he doing to me?

The timing couldn't be worse! I had all I could handle right now with The Grand struggling, Evelyn hounding me and Jake pressuring me to set a wedding date. Parker Blackwell and his antics were the last thing I needed at a time like this. If I could avoid him for the rest of the weekend, by checkout time on Sunday he'd be long gone before Jake came home and hopefully before I turned into a stark raving maniac.

As soon as the thought crossed my mind I knew it would be impossible, and the real reason was hard to admit. I was inexplicably and undeniably drawn to him. I always have been. The dynamic between us was like a tiny spark that didn't take much to spread into a raging inferno. It was always there, but all those years ago we were too young; too inexperienced to recognize it. He was frustrating, infuriating, but he ignited something inside me that no other man had ever reached. It was deep and sexual, and it was frightening.

Desperate, I dug through my purse for my cell and called Nina again. This time I was instantly relieved when I heard her voice on the other end.

"Nina, where the hell have you been? I hope you can talk. Oh my God! I don't even know where to start!"

"Okay, I'm here. I'm sorry. I was at Leslie's. She had another episode, because Trina Lavonne went missing. You know how she gets when something happens to her cats. Anyway, what the hell is going on? Are you okay?"

I knew exactly what she meant. Leslie was Nina's mom, and she was a crazy cat lady; a childlike hippy who never quite grew up. I often wondered if she took one too many psychedelic trips in the '70s. Who knows? Poor Nina had all she could do to look after her. Still, I envied their relationship sometimes. Better to have a mother who was bat shit crazy than no mother at all.

I knew everything about Nina, and she knew everything about me. We grew up together in this small community since grade school. Oddly enough, she hated the beach, well really she "revered the power of the sun," and she would go on and on ranting about skin cancer and the chemicals in sunscreen, but that never stopped me from dragging her along on all my adventures. She would drench us both in organic sunscreen and remind me every hour to reapply. She was quite a mother hen and a spiritual guru thanks to her mother, always talking about auras and chakras and things I would know nothing about if it wasn't for her. I loved her so much. Just hearing her voice soothed me.

"Nina, this is bad! This is so fucking bad. I need your help, so listen close. You're never going to believe who's staying at The Grand."

"Who? You're scaring me now."

"Parker Blackwell…" Nina fell silent. She knew the history. She knew how I felt about him and how much I hated him when he left. "Please say something!"

The sound of her dragging in a deep breath filled the receiver, and I knew she was going to get all spiritual on me, but I didn't mind. Right now I needed something, anything to help me make sense of it all.

I continued, "He's here, and he's fucking gorgeous, Nina. I mean he's tall and built and his eyes…he mesmerized me with his eyes, his smell. I don't know what to do! I want to hate him, but…"

"Oh, Lo, this *is* bad! This is so fucking bad! Where's Jake? Is he here?"

"No, he's working out of town."

"Fuck! I have a bad feeling about this. Please listen to me. You have to stay away from Parker. Do you hear what

I'm saying? Jake is the one for you, Lo. Your auras are perfectly matched. Leslie is never wrong about these things. I'm telling you."

Her ominous tone concerned me. I mean, I fully expected her to be pro-Jake, but the fact that she was adamantly anti-Parker surprised me. "Nina, I know! I agree with everything you're saying, but I don't know how to explain this. It's different. This has never happened to me before. Not even with Jake. There's something about him, Nina, some connection to my past that's drawing me to him."

"Okay, wait a minute. Remember your last session with Leslie? Your heart chakra was out of whack, right?"

"Nina, please. How can that have anything to do with this? I think I should have Leslie read my cards. Maybe she can see something that we can't." Although I didn't get too caught up in Leslie's physic abilities, she was right about my mom's diagnosis, and that's something I'll never forget. I still had her read my cards once in a while, especially when I had more questions than answers.

Nina's voice became stern. "Okay, a reading couldn't hurt, but you're not listening to me. When your heart chakra is unbalanced, more energy is directed to your head chakra where your memories live. Lo, you're not feeling clear emotions right now."

She obviously had no idea what I was feeling. Maybe I didn't elaborate enough. "Oh, I'm feeling, Nina. I'm feeling every cell in my body being pulled toward him like a magnet, every nerve ending standing at attention, every thought being erased but him. Is that enough detail for you? Do you get it now?"

"Yes, I get it! You want to throw caution to the wind and fuck him like an animal, right? But I'm talking about the *why* here, Lo. These feelings are coming from your mind, your memories; not your heart."

"Yeah, I guess. But I just don't know where this came from or what to do with it all. I've never felt this way before," I quietly confessed. "It scares me, Nina."

"Just stay away from him, Lo. You have to."

"That's impossible. He's going to be here until Sunday, and Tom and Mary are here, too."

Her drawn out sigh was worth a thousand words.

"Okay, how about this? I'll be careful," I promised, "I'll try not to be alone with him."

"I hope you know what you're doing, Lo. I have a bad feeling about this. Please, please be careful."

Nina loved me, and I couldn't ask for a more caring friend, but I couldn't help but laugh at her deadly serious demeanor. "I will. Now I should get some sleep to help balance my whacked out chakras."

"Good idea. Call me tomorrow? I'll be worried."

"Sure thing."

Still feeling restless after all the talk about chakras and auras, I rolled over, grabbed my laptop and Googled "pheromones." It could be pheromones, right? I mean I'd never felt the uncontrollable urge to jump on a man and wrap my legs around him before in my life. Yet every time I looked at Parker I could barely think of anything else. All he had to do was breathe the same air as me and I felt my self-control crumbling, and the things he could do with just a touch were obscene. I screamed into my pillow to release the frustration. *What is happening to me?*

Okay, where was I? Pheromones. Right. Well, according to some websites there is much controversy over whether or not they actually exist. *Huh! Someone should have been conducting a study in my parking lot a few*

minutes ago!

After a little more searching my thoughts were

confirmed when I found an interesting tidbit in *The*

Smithsonian Magazine. Apparently, if a wild female boar

gets a whiff of the pheromones emitted by her male

counterpart "she'll present her rear to the male." *Ugh! Can*

he really reduce me to such a primal level?

I wondered where he was right now. The Parker

Blackwell I used to know was far too used to getting his

way. He must be furious, or maybe trying to find Blondie's

number. The thought made my stomach turn.

With visuals of wild boars, primal instincts, chakras

and auras swirling in my brain, I undressed and flung

myself across the bed wishing I could rewind the day and

somehow avoid the fateful meeting that had my insides

tangled up in knots.

While I was deep in thought I must have missed the footsteps on the stairs, but the knock on my door sent my heart pounding through my chest. I grabbed my dress from the floor and held it against me as I peeked through the peep hole. *Shit! It's Mary and Tom!*

"Lauren, honey, are you there?" Her voice was full of motherly concern.

Still clutching my dress with one hand, I opened the door just a crack and felt my face flush as I saw the looks on their faces.

"I'm so sorry Mary. I wasn't feeling well, and I had to turn in early. I asked Parker to let you know. Have you seen him?"

Mary and Tom exchanged glances. Then Mary gave a knowing smile.

I knew it! He must be with Blondie, or some other warm body that fell for his alarming good looks and boyish charm. Why does that sound like sarcastic regret, Lo?

"It's all right, dear. We just wanted to make sure you were okay." Mary nudged Tom.

He sputtered a bit then cleared his throat, cupping his hand in front of his mouth. They looked stunned, but strangely amused.

"Yes, we hope you're feeling better tomorrow. Mary planned a wine tasting tour for us. Go ahead and get some rest. We'll meet you in the lobby at noon."

Their reaction puzzled me. Then suddenly the fear of spending another day with Parker sent a million crazy excuses spinning wildly through my brain. Before I could choose the perfect one, Mary tugged Tom's hand, and the two of them walked away arm in arm.

Fuck! Could this get any better? The truth is I didn't have the heart to lie to them, and I didn't really want to. But the thought of another round with Parker was, was…

I slid the covers over me and tried to block the thought of this night and that man out of my mind. I needed to sleep on it. Things would seem clearer in the morning.

Just as I was drifting off, Jake's ringtone came blaring from my cell phone.

"Hey, were you sleeping?"

The sound of his voice made me smile. "Not yet. How's the project going?"

"It's going."

I could tell from his tone it wasn't going well. "That doesn't sound too convincing. What's going on?"

Jake is a commercial project manager in charge of several trades. He's under constant pressure to meet next to impossible deadlines, but he's well equipped to handle it. He's a technical guy, straight-laced, organized, and dependable. In many ways he's the complete opposite of Parker Blackwell.

A twinge of guilt washed over me as I listened to Jake explain why he wouldn't be able to make it home until late Sunday night. I wanted to tell him what happened, but I knew it wasn't the right time.

"So, I guess I'll see you Sunday night then?" He finished.

My mind had wandered from our conversation. Suddenly thoughts of Jake, the Jake I fell in love with flashed through my mind. *What happened to us?*

"Ah, yeah. My place?"

"Absolutely. See you then." With those final words he hung up the phone.

I knew he wasn't one for pleasantries. He would often hang up without saying goodbye or I love you, but this time the disappointment gnawed at me a little more than usual. I needed him, and his abrupt departure left me feeling even more alone.

Five

YOU CAN'T GO BACK

As soon as my eyes opened images of what happened the night before replayed in my head. I needed coffee, a shower and a plan in that order. I headed for the kitchen imagining what the day would bring.

There was one thing I was sure of - Parker Blackwell was dangerous. The emotions that stirred inside of me when I was close to him were frightening. My body began to recall how his hands and mouth had me on the edge, but my mind quickly stopped it from going there.

I remembered Nina's warning and decided I would dress much less provocatively around him. After all, I didn't want to give him any indication that I was interested in anything more than his friendship or invite him to repeat what happened the night before. Because, honestly if there was a next time I wasn't sure I could resist him.

I went to the closet and chose a girlish sundress. No cleavage, not too much leg, and definitely no sexy shoes. Yep, simple flat flip-flops would do. Oh, and a ponytail. I don't know why, but guys hate ponytails. Jake does anyway. Yep! Today I would be "plain Jane" as my mom would say.

Proud of myself, I strutted off to the shower. He might be bigger than me now, stronger than me, but there's one thing I was sure of—he wasn't smarter than me. I was going to enjoy the day with Mary and Tom and keep Parker in check. I wouldn't let him push my buttons. Nope, today was going to be a great day.

I rounded the corner to the lobby feeling confident that I could keep his pheromones in check; especially with my new plain Jane look which I was pulling off flawlessly.

Tom and Mary were waiting on the bench by the door, and their faces lit up when they saw me. I looked around quickly my heart beating faster. *Where is he?*

Reading the look on my face, Mary spoke up, "He went to get us coffee, dear. He'll be right back."

God! Am I that obvious? Don't be a wild boar, Lo!

"Oh, who?" I feigned indifference, and Mary smiled.

Right on cue Parker entered looking just as deliciously seductive as he did last night…*with his head leaning back against the wall. Stop it, Lo!*

"Tom this one's for you." He reached in front of me and handed Tom his to-go cup.

"Mary, your chai tea." Mary smiled up at him sweetly.

"And for you, Lauren, vanilla latte. I don't know what you like, but I'm sure vanilla is a safe bet," he winked at me as he handed me my cup. "Oh, and here's your room key. I forgot to give it back to you last night."

All the color drained from my face, and my mouth dropped open. I glanced quickly at Mary and Tom. Their eyes grew wide, and their expressions were priceless.

I forced a stiff smile and replied through gritted teeth, "Why thank you Parker. I see you're just as thoughtful as ever this morning. And thank you for walking me to my room last night. I was so sick, it took everything I had to not vomit all over your expensive shoes. I must have rushed to the bathroom so fast that I didn't even remember to ask for my room key back."

Bastard! Nice save, Lo. I sure hope they believed you.

Mary and Tom were looking at us, and I could tell by their expressions they weren't sure what to make of our little exchange.

I changed the subject quickly, "Are we ready to go?"

"I'm ready," Mary sighed. "I've been waiting to take this tour for fifteen years. This is the first time Tom agreed to it."

She pulled a brochure from her purse. "Our first stop will be Chateau Fontaine, and Parker volunteered to be our designated driver for the day. Isn't that nice, Lo?"

"Yes. He's such a nice guy that Parker. A perfect gentleman really," I managed.

He eyed me suspiciously. I knew he was trying to get me to engage, but I had outsmarted him for now. He must be disappointed, confused even. *Poor guy!*

Tom held the door, and I followed Mary out into the sunlit sidewalk. I hoped he would get the picture. I'm not going to join him in his silly little dance today. But when Jim, our valet, pulled up with his car, I almost caved.

I've seen plenty of fancy sports cars up here, and I knew exactly what kind of arrogant rich boys were behind the wheel--the kind that used daddy's bankroll to pay for them. *The bastard drives a Mercedes! And, not just any Mercedes. I don't even recognize the model!*

When Jim got out it was clear that even he was impressed. "This is one beautiful car, sir. I've never seen one like it, and I've parked a lot of 'em over the years."

Parker was instantly intrigued. "Thanks. Yeah, she's a beauty! A Maybach Landaulet to be exact."

Letting out a long low whistle, Jim opened the back door for Mary and continued talking about the car. "Bet you got her after winning the World Poker Tour in Australia, huh?"

"Nope, after that one I bought the Aston Martin One-77, but I thought the Mercedes would be more comfortable for my passengers." Parker said as he smirked at me.

My mind was clinging to the words *'World Poker Tour'. Parker is a poker player?*

I should've known he wouldn't choose a professional career, like a doctor or lawyer, although his parents' money could have paid for either. But a poker player? By the looks of this car, he must be quite successful, unless his mommy was funding everything. I couldn't help myself. I was desperate to find out.

It took all the determination I had to keep my mouth shut as we drove up the coast. Mary took the liberty of filling in the silence, and her endless chatter provided a welcome relief. The longer we drove, the lighter the mood became. Eventually, we were all laughing comfortably and talking about all sorts of things.

At one point, Mary was telling us about a funny argument that occurred between Sarah and her new husband over the number of children they each wanted. Everyone was laughing, and from the corner of my eye, I saw Parker looking at me. Things were going well so fa, better than expected, really, that is until he suddenly changed the direction of the conversation.

Looking in the rear view mirror he asked Tom and Mary, "Did you know *our* Lauren is engaged? Tell us all about your fiancé, Lo. What's he like? I'll bet he's a real *swell* guy."

Our Lauren? Swell guy? Since when does Parker say swell? I knew exactly what he was trying to do.

I could hear the excitement in Mary's voice from the backseat. "Lo, you never mentioned you were engaged! Congratulations, dear! Where is the lucky fella? I'd love to meet him."

"Yes, where is the lucky fella, Lo?" Parker mocked as he looked at me with those mischievous, piercing green eyes.

I'll be damned if I'm going to let this asshole slam Jake! He couldn't measure up if he tried! Be careful, don't take the bait, Lo!

I forced a smile and laughed casually. "His name is Jake," I added, looking Parker straight in the eye, "And, he's amazing. Too bad he's out of town this weekend. I know he'd love to meet you, too." Rolling my eyes I returned my attention to the view out the passenger window.

"Well, too bad for him, huh? I mean that he's out of town." The corners of his mouth curled slightly when he smiled. And then it happened. The air seemed still, and I had to crack my window to breathe. Pheromones. *Damn him! I mean can he really use them on demand?*

When he looked my way again I cautiously flipped him the bird so that our passengers couldn't see. His eyes grew wide as he clutched his chest in fake shock. *He was impossible!*

"Enough about me, Parker. Who's the lucky lady in your life these days? Or, should I say ladies?"

"I travel too much to have a *lady,"* his voice trailed off at the end sending a subtle message to me.

I knew exactly what he meant. There were many and probably none of them were ladies. The thought made me squirm in my seat and had me adjusting my seatbelt to get comfortable. *Time to change the subject!*

The sign announcing we had arrived at the first winery was a welcome relief. I exhaled deeply as I exited the car and smiled at the sight of Mary anxiously tugging Tom toward the building. I started to follow after them when Parker's voice stopped me in my tracks.

"Lo, wait a minute."

"Yeah, I'll wait a minute all right!" I spun around to face him, taking the room key out of my purse and tossing it at him. "What kind of stunt was that anyway? I'm sure some woman at my hotel is hoping this is a sign you'll be back for round two tonight, huh?"

"It's my room key, Lo. It was just a joke. Mary was asking me fifty questions about where I was last night. I think she suspected I was with you. So, it was too easy. I'm sorry. I should've thought about it I guess, but that's not what I wanted to talk about."

My stomach did a back flip and tied itself into a million double knots. I was afraid to turn around. As I watched the door close behind Mary and Tom I knew I had to face him--all six feet of deliciously sculptured, dangerously fuckable, and extremely frustrating Parker Blackwell. It took everything I had not to want him more than my next breath.

"Look, Parker, if this is about last night I…"

"What do you mean *if,* Lo? It's more than just last night. It's the way you've made me feel ever since I met you. The way you feel when you're with me."

My heart was slamming in my chest. I couldn't deny how much I wanted him. *What the fuck did he want from me?*

"The way *I* feel? Being with you is torture. Everything's a game to you, Parker. Whatever we had, or whatever we were when we were kids, it's still the same. I mean it's different. Fuck, I don't know what I mean anymore! What I do know is that you left me. You left me when I needed you the most, and now we can't go back."

Frustration got the best of me and as much as I wanted to explain, I couldn't find the right words. Then it came to me. "We're all grown up now. I'm a business owner.

You're a poker player. I'm engaged, and you're still putting notches in your bedpost."

Parker was looking at the ground, his brow creased. He looked deep in thought, and I could see the storm brewing as his eyes darkened. I held my breath and braced myself for the backlash, but instead his voice was surprisingly calm. Almost too calm.

"Lo, I understand why you'd think that, and in a lot of ways you're right. I can't deny the number of women I've been through. With my looks, personality, and profession it kind of goes with the territory. But honestly none of them have ever challenged me like you do. Not one. I know what you need, Lo, and I want to give it to you. I should have never left you back then. If you'd give me a chance, I could make it up to you. I want to give you everything. We understand each other."

Things were moving too fast, and my mind was whirling. I tried to steer the conversation away from what we both knew was hanging in the balance. The things left unsaid, the chemistry, the unresolved. "They haven't challenged you? How could that be possible? I mean with *your* looks, personality, and profession?" I fired back, covering my face then shoving my hands deep into my hair.

I couldn't look at him, but I felt his eyes studying me. That's when I realized I had two reactions whenever I was near him. I either wanted to run away or fight. Fight him. Fight myself. It was fight or flight. All or nothing, and when we engaged like this, I had to resist the urge to rip his clothes off and unleash my pent up frustration on him. He was like a shot of tequila-- tempting, strong and unpredictable. Would the initial burn be worth the invincible feeling waiting on the other side, or would I just lose control?

"You're right, Lo. Some things are the same. You still put your hands in your hair when you're frustrated. You hide your face when you don't want me to see what's going on behind those beautiful yellow eyes of yours. You're still my fantasy, and we're still like gasoline and fire together. So, I have to know, does this man you plan to marry really know you? Does he make you passionate, push you until you're ready to unravel?" He paused as if he were waiting for me to answer. "I already know the truth. If he did you wouldn't be here right now."

"You have no idea, Parker! Jake loves me. He wants what's best for me, and he's not going anywhere. You on the other hand? You're a gamble. You always have been, and whether it's seven, ten or twenty years from now you always will be."

"You're settling, Lo. I can see it all over your face."

"That's the best you can come up with? Well, I'm sorry you've grown bored with having one meaningless encounter after the next, but whatever twisted idea you have about me and you it's never going to work! I'm not here for your entertainment, and I don't base my life on challenges, silly games, or bets for that matter. We'd be crazy to think that we could last more than one hour together let alone a lifetime! And you think I'm settling? That I'd be so much better off with you? Do these lines really work for you, Parker? Please! You'll never know what I need!"

I fully expected the backlash at any moment, but once again nothing. In fact, the mischievous smile was back. "Who said anything about a lifetime? Let's try an hour first."

Before I knew what was happening, he grabbed me around the waist and hoisted me over his shoulder.

"Put me down!" I screamed pounding his back.

I hoped someone in the parking lot would witness my abduction and stop him. He must have thought someone might see us too and quickly set me back on my feet, dragging me by the hand instead.

"Come on." His voice was stern.

Trying to pull myself free, I screamed through gritted teeth, "Let me go!"

"One hour." His calm demand sent shivers down my back. His intentions weren't clear, but I couldn't find the words to defend myself, and somewhere deep inside I didn't want to.

On shaky legs, I followed him around the corner into the shadow of the imposing rustic barn near the parking lot. My nostrils were flaring from the rush of emotions, and somehow even in the eighty degree heat I had goose bumps.

When we were safely out of view I took in the scene. A small grove of trees lined the top of the hill overlooking the vineyard in front of us, and the sun beamed through the branches creating shadows all around. We were alone.

He released my hand slowly as if he was worried I might run the minute he let go. I was frozen. The battle inside of me was raging, but when I looked up at him I knew instantly that something about him had changed. His face was relaxed, calm even. His hand caressed my cheek lightly, before gently sweeping my bangs away from my eyes I wanted to cling to him. Everything inside of me wanted to open up and let him in.

"I've always loved to look at you, Lo. I almost forgot how beautiful you are."

My cheeks burned hot, fueled by the delicious mixture of anger and anticipation. His touch made me lick my lips instinctively, and I tried to look away.

"Don't hide your face from me. I never want you to feel like you have to hide from me."

The tenderness in his voice touched places deep inside of me. Places that I had kept locked away for a long time. I looked up at his face, so filled with quiet admiration, and the sun seemed to shine around him like a halo. He cupped my chin in his hands and brushed his lips softly over mine. I closed my eyes, sure he could hear my heartbeat. Our lips pressed together, slowly parting, lingering, and melting my resistance and uncertainty until I felt myself matching his rhythm.

He stepped closer into me, pinning my body against the rough cool wood of the barn. I held my hands against his chest, afraid of what would happen if I dropped my guard completely. The solid strength of his body felt unyielding beneath my fingertips. He wrapped his hand in my ponytail gently pulling my lips from his before blazing a trail across my cheek and down to the most sensitive part of my neck. I was lost in him. The smell of him, and the familiarity of him, brought me back to a time when life was perfect, before my world came crashing down and everything changed forever--back to the picture I still carried in my mind.

Cracks started to form in the wall that shielded me from all the sadness and fear until tears spilled through my eyelashes. I didn't want him to stop, but I couldn't control the overwhelming emotions from pouring out.

"Lo, what's wrong?" His eyes mixed with desire and confusion searched mine as he wiped my tears away like they were delicate butterflies and pulled me into him tight.

"I'm sorry," I whispered, "I just feel so..."

"What? What do you feel, Lo? Tell me."

Standing there with him I felt like I was twelve-years-old again when my dog, Zoey, had to be put to sleep. I had a hole in my heart that I couldn't explain. My insides felt hollow. I remembered my dad pushing away the tear soaked strands of hair that clung to my cheeks and wrapping me in his arms so tight. We both knew there was nothing he could do to fix it, but having his strength and love all around me as my heart overflowed was something I'll never forget.

It's been a long time since I've allowed myself to feel anything so freely, probably since shortly after my dad passed away. I tried to keep everything locked inside; especially from Jake. He had a hard time dealing with emotions, but I knew he did the best he could. Raised with a strict military father and a docile obedient mother, emotions had no place in his upbringing. The times I did bare my soul to him, he nearly shut down. There were nights I spent sobbing while lying next to him in bed, and all he could do was pull me close and hold me next to him. Somehow it was enough. It had to be, but lately that connection was gone, and I felt lonely and afraid.

"If I pushed you too far, I'm sorry," came Parker's comforting whisper.

Trying to calm my ragged breathing enough to speak, I closed my eyes while he waited patiently. Once I regained some composure, what came out of my mouth surprised even me.

"Parker, before I saw you again I thought my life was just fine, but you've only been here two days, and I'm questioning everything I thought was right. I'm wondering if it was all just an illusion that I created to avoid dealing with the truth."

Feeling like I'd just made a life changing confession, I exhaled deeply. His silence was unnerving. The muscles in his jaw tensed, and his eyes were full of uncertainty.

Swallowing hard he grabbed my hand. "What is the truth?"

My eyes dropped to the ground. I couldn't look at him, but he wouldn't let me off that easily. I felt his fingers brush my chin before lifting it, bringing my eyes back to meet his. "The truth is that nothing is okay. The Grandview, things with Jake…" I squeaked out the words and watched his face tighten with worry as his jaw flinched again.

"I know things with Jake aren't perfect," anger flashed over his face, "but what's going on with The Grand?"

The more I spoke, the more I realized this wasn't the time or place to complicate things between us. I had already revealed too much to this man. I was too vulnerable. I tried to think of a way to avoid answering. *Why am I confiding in this practical stranger? Am I really this needy?*

I pushed him aside gently and took a few steps forward. *Inhale. Exhale.* I tried to absorb the serenity of the view as I wiped my face and smoothed my hands over my clothes. I needed to shake these feelings. I needed to get back to Tom and Mary where I was safe from making matters worse.

I swallowed, trying hard to sound shaky, "We should get back before they wonder what happened to us."

Disappointment spread across his face, but he must have sensed not to push me any farther. "Yeah, I guess we should."

I was relieved.

"But you know…" the mischievous grin was back, "I could keep you right here for hours."

"Really?" I replied clearing my throat, my smile returning.

"Yes, really. The minute I saw that ponytail this morning all kinds of crazy thoughts went through my mind. You haven't seen half of them yet." Dark desire burned in his eyes, and I briefly remembered the look from the night on the sidewalk in front of The Grand.

The ponytail? I would love to see what he had in mind...

"The deal was one hour," I remind him playfully, "And although you've only kept me here for about thirty minutes now," I said looking at my watch, "I think its best that we get back to the others. They'll be worried." I was torn. Part of me wanted this moment to last. I wanted to feel the comfort of his arms around me, and the warmth of his chest against my cheek.

"Kept you here, huh? From what I see you aren't restrained...although that can be arranged if you like to play rough."

And just like that the intensity returned. I pulled away, and he reeled me back in. It was a game of temptation and anticipation. I wanted to play along, but I knew I shouldn't.

I was afraid to think of where it might lead. No, I knew where it would lead. Instead I turned and started walking toward the entrance.

We made our way back to the group in silence, Parker walking slightly behind me. When we finally met up with Tom and Mary they were just finishing up the tour.

"Where have you two been?" Mary asked cautiously. "You've missed out on all the fun."

"Sorry to worry you, Aunt Mary. Lauren and I went for a walk, and the view was incredible! Wouldn't you agree, Lo?"

I shot Parker a look of disbelief before trying to explain.

"Yes, we had a wonderful time catching up."

Tom put his hand on Mary's shoulder as if to stop her from prying any further. "Well, that's great, you two. You didn't miss much anyway." Mary glared at him, and he chuckled.

Taking the opportunity to change the subject, Parker quickly interrupted. "I'll go get the car if you're ready to head to our next stop."

As he walked away, my gaze instinctively followed. Everything about him screamed confidence, experience, and pure sex. *What am I doing with him? Am I entertaining some unfulfilled fantasy, or am I fooling myself into believing there could be something more?*

The rest of the day was perfect. Parker tried to lure me away several times, playfully pointing out places we could go to escape when the others weren't looking. Between his antics and Mary's stories, I laughed until my stomach hurt.

The mood between us had relaxed. It felt like a valve had opened relieving the pressure that had kept us at odds for so long. The sexual tension lurking just below the surface was undeniable, but things seemed kinder, lighter.

On the drive back, Mary suggested that we meet for dinner on the patio at The Grand. They would be leaving at check-out in the morning, and the idea seemed like the perfect ending to our weekend together.

I went back to my room to freshen up, and called down to the bar to reserve a table. It was Saturday night, and the same band was playing again. Anticipating another full house, I could hear the excitement in Steve's voice as he assured me that everything was under control.

Fully satisfied that The Grand might really be making a comeback, I hung up the phone with a smile. However, the butterflies tingling in my stomach as I thought about saying goodbye to Parker reminded me that things were far from under control.

Thoughts of Parker consumed me. Our indescribable attraction had suddenly turned my world upside-down. Every part of me wanted him. Like an addict, the high he had me on was insatiable. That's the only way to describe it. I felt like I'd tried a dangerous drug for the first time. I knew I should stay away. I knew I had to be careful not to let this feeling take control of me, but the high was too powerful, and it was only a matter of time before it drew me in deep.

My chest flooded with anxiety when I heard my phone beep. It was a text from Jake.

"The job is still behind schedule. I'm staying to work through the night. I'll see you in the morning."

Tossing the phone on the table like it just bit me, I gave it one last look before walking out the door. Parker would be gone in the morning. Jake would be home, and things would be back to normal again. My face felt warm with guilt and shame, but I quickly pushed these feelings out of my mind. For now, I was chasing the high, and it scared me to admit that I would do anything to feel it one more time.

Six

INTO TEMPTATION

As soon as I opened the door, I came face to face with Parker. "Oh my God! You scared the hell out of me!" I shrieked stumbling backward into the room.

"Glad to see I have that effect on you, Lo." His lips curled in that delicious way that sent warm tingles up my spine.

Feeling panicked, I blurted out the only thing that came to mind. "What are you doing here? I thought we were meeting for dinner in a few minutes?"

"We are, but I wanted to talk to you first. Alone."

Alone. I didn't expect to be alone with him again so soon. My heart jumped at the thought.

"Sounds serious. You want to come in for a minute? But just for a minute. Tom and Mary are waiting," I reminded him as my body protested silently.

When he followed me in I felt his eyes on me. I retreated to the far end of the kitchen and positioned my back against the counter waiting for his explanation. My pulse raced when I glanced over at the dangerous proximity of my king size bed.

Before I knew what was happening, he quickly closed the gap between us. His hands pushed my dress up as he lifted me onto the counter with his body positioned squarely between my legs.

I bit my lip hard as the heat of his hands on my bare thighs sent sparks of energy pulsing and swirling through my body. He lowered his head touching his lips to my neck, increasing the pressure slowly, deliberately. His fingers massaged my thighs working on a path ever closer to the spot where I longed to feel his touch. Easing my head back I closed my eyes and shamelessly opened myself to him.

His lips found mine, and our tongues slid together eagerly as his fingers finally reached their goal--gently brushing over the thin satin barrier of my panties. His other hand tugged at the front of my dress, expertly exposing my breasts. I wrapped my arms around his shoulders and inhaled sharply as his warm mouth captured one hard peak and then the other creating a delicious throbbing sensation between my legs. Arching into him, I moaned and his name escaped my lips.

He leaned his forehead against mine as if to clear his mind and whispered, "Shh…Lo, just listen for a minute please." His fingers retreated, tracing lines at the hem of my dress as he spoke, making it hard for me to concentrate. I squeezed my eyes shut, trying to fight off the urge to touch him. Struggling with the need for him to rip my clothes off and take me on the kitchen counter, my thighs remained spread wide silently inviting him to take more.

My body tensed with anticipation when I opened my eyes again to find him staring at me, and I watched as his tongue flicked over his bottom lip before he continued. My finger instinctively traced the path his tongue had made, and his eyes narrowed and his brow creased as he winced as if he were in pain.

"I want to carry you to your bed claim your body in every imaginable way, leaving no doubt that you belong to me," he said, his voice low and raspy as he grabbed my hand and squeezed. "Don't make this harder for me than it already is. There are things we need to talk about first."

He brought me so painfully close to the edge. My body willed him to keep going. "I want you too, Parker. I think we both need to…give in. We both need closure so we can move on with our lives."

"Christ, Lo! Is that what you think this is about? Moving on? Closure?" He pulled away turning his back to me as his hands fisted angrily in his hair.

"What do you want from me, Parker? I'm confused. Against every moral fiber in my soul, I've just admitted that I want to have sex with you, to close this chapter once and for all. And that makes you angry? Am I missing something here?" I sat up and tugged my dress back into place.

He stormed around the kitchen his jaw flinching. "Fuck, yes. It makes me angry! I thought coming here would be a mistake, but I'm glad I did. I've never had this kind of connection with anyone before. I wasn't even sure if it would still be there, and facing either possibility scared the hell out of me. But the moment I saw you again I knew it did, and I knew I couldn't lose it this time."

I couldn't breathe. My eyes were fixed on him, still pacing. Lowering his voice he continued, "Seven years ago when I found out your mom was sick, that she might die," he paused, swallowing hard. My body went stiff when I realized where he was going. "I panicked, Lo. I knew there was nothing I could do to fix it. I knew you were about to go through the worst pain you had ever felt in your life, and there wasn't a fucking thing I could do to change it, but I was just a kid. I didn't know what do, so I ran, and I never looked back. I have never forgiven myself for leaving you alone when you needed me most."

I almost choked on the lump forming in my throat. I've needed to hear those words for so long. Pushing myself abruptly off the counter and straitening my skirt, I turned my back to him so he couldn't see my face. I squeezed my eyes shut and willed the memories to leave my brain. Then, not sure if I could ever truly forgive him but desperately wanting to, I lied. "Parker, it's in the past now. It's over."

"No, it's not over. You had the perfect life, Lo, the perfect family, friends, The Grandview. I always wanted to be a part of that in some way. Me on the other hand, I had nothing without Tom and Mary. Through the endless parade of stepparents and moving from state to state they were the closest thing to a real family I ever had, and so were you. When everything was falling apart I did too. I cracked under the pressure, and instead of holding on I just let it all go. It was the biggest mistake of my life, Lo, and I'm not about to make it again."

Make it again? What did he mean by that? His words vibrated through my brain as I spun around to meet his intense gaze. "I missed you Parker. I'm still mad as hell at you, but I missed you. I don't think I ever let go of that either, but like I said it's over now. Let's just move on. Isn't that what you want?"

Anger flashed over his face, and he almost roared. "I want you to stop being so proud and let me help you! I'm not about to stand by and watch you lose all that you have left, especially not when there's something I can do to stop it. Jesus! Do I have to spell it out, Lo? I found out just how deeply The Grand's in trouble. I know about the situation with Evelyn, and I want you to let me help."

I held my balled fists at my sides. Frustrated, I screamed back, "So that's what this is all about? Some seven year guilt trip you need to resolve? I don't need your help, Parker Blackwell! I lived without it then, and I can live without it now!"

"I deserved that, but I knew you'd be stubborn. You're fucking impossible. You know that? Why won't you take my help? It's just money, and I have plenty of it. Call it a loan if that helps you swallow your fucking pride. Call it whatever you want. I couldn't live with myself if you lost this place."

"I'm not losing anything!" I dug my fingers into the edge of the countertop, resisting the urge to lash out at him. I wanted this conversation to be over, and I couldn't wait to get away from him. Several minutes passed in silence.

His voice was barely a whisper, but I heard exactly what he said, "I've always loved you, Lo."

My head dropped down from the weight of the overwhelming emotions those words stirred inside of me. The memories of my mom and dad, their deaths, his absence, his return. It was all too much to bare.

"How can you love me, Parker? We don't even know each other anymore. Sex and love are two different things." Even as the words left my mouth I wondered if in some inexplicable way I loved him, too.

"Believe me, Lo. I know the difference between sex and love. They're two different things in my world. I think you can have one without the other, but not many people find both."

Now I was pacing, too. Both of us, pacing around the kitchen, saying the things that we waited seven long years to say. "Seriously? With your wild and free lifestyle you're going to stand here and educate me about love and sex? Don't you think that's ironic?"

"There are things you don't know about me, Lo. My lifestyle is fucked up compared to most people. I take pleasure when I want it, and I give it when I choose. Beyond that, I've never felt the need to complicate things with love. You're the only woman I'd ever consider sharing something more with."

I was seething with anger. Apparently he thought I was some charity case, a damsel in distress that he could save in order to alleviate his own guilty conscience. "Are you done?" I asked coldly.

Judging by the look on his face, my clipped response caught him off guard. "For now."

"You must think I'm some naïve little girl who still believes in fairytales. Well, let me set the record straight. After losing my mom, my best friend and my dad all to reasons outside my control, I stopped believing in fairytales a long time ago. So if that's all, Parker, then I have to go. Mary and Tom are waiting."

With that, I turned and walked outside leaving him standing alone in my kitchen.

Seven

ULTERIOR MOTIVES

I had exactly five minutes to regain my composure before dinner. No matter how difficult it would be, I had to shove the conversation with Parker to the back of my mind. I'd have time to analyze it later. Having made up my mind, I took a deep breath as I walked out onto the patio.

The edges of the blue and white striped umbrellas covering the tables flapped gently in the warm lake breeze. It was the perfect night for dining outside, and I was determined to make the best of it. Forcing a smile, I looked around and noticed every table was full inside and out. I stopped at the bar to check in, but with everyone hustling they barely had a moment to spare.

"Hey there," Steve called over his shoulder. "I thought I told you we had this under control?"

"Yeah, yeah. I know, but you know me. I couldn't stay away if I tried."

"Yep, that sounds about right. Okay, so here's the scoop. We'll have three bartenders, six servers and three door guys tonight. I changed the special from prime rib to porterhouse after we ran out earlier. Current wait list is twenty minutes. We have a reservation for fifteen at eight o'clock, and the band will start again at nine. Are you satisfied?"

"Yes, very. Now if only you and Matt could learn to make the ladies swoon like Tom Cruise in *Cocktail* we'll make a fortune," I quipped as I rolled my eyes.

Matt piped in as his fingers dashed over the keys on the cash register. "Yeah, and then you could hire some

Coyote Ugly girls to dance on the bar and we'd really have a show!"

Steve laughed and shook his head. "See what you started? Now I'm ordering you to get out of here. And, by the way, it's really nice to see you smile again. Now go enjoy your company, Lo, really."

I made my way to the patio wishing everything in life could be as easy as dealing with my bar staff. They were like family to me, and they kept this place going through good times and bad. Now if I could just keep the rooms and the tavern full, I might be able to reward them with more than just words.

Mary and Tom came downstairs right on time, but I noticed the worried look on Mary's face right away. Looking past them, my heart fluttered in my chest the moment I realized Parker wasn't there. I tried to hide my disappointment as my eyes went from the stairs to the tavern door waiting for him to appear, but it was useless.

When we sat down Mary started to explain. "It's such a gorgeous night. It's too bad Parker won't be joining us."

I blinked at her expectantly, hovering on her every word. I expected him to be here with that same arrogant smile on his face. I thought we'd be able to keep things civil enough to get through dinner for Mary and Tom's sake. I never considered the possibility of him not showing, and it gave me a strange unsettled feeling.

Mary continued on, "He stopped by our room a few minutes ago to let us know he had some business to take care of in town. Something about a meeting with an attorney that couldn't wait." She waived her hand gracefully as though dismissing his excuse. "You never know what that man has up his sleeve. He's always thinking about business even when he's on vacation," she continued, "Sorry, Lo, it seemed like the two of you were getting on so well, too."

I felt like I'd been kicked in the stomach. *How stupid can you be, Lo? Did you honestly believe he would come back for more?* I tried to smile, but I could hardly contain the nauseous feeling in my stomach. "Business, huh? I wonder if the attorney is a female. I mean with his looks, personality and profession, I'm sure it happens all the time."

I could tell by the looks on Tom and Mary's faces that my snarky comment caught them by surprise, and I immediately regretted opening my mouth. Laughing nervously I tried to shake it off. "That Parker! I guess some things never change!"

I hid my face behind the menu to collect my thoughts. "So, where were we? Our special tonight is porterhouse. What sounds good to you, Mary? How about an appetizer?"

I waited, hoping that my clumsy attempt at changing the subject had worked. After a few seconds, I peeked over the top of the menu just in time to see the two of them looking at each other as if they were communicating in some secret unspoken language that people only learn after being married for many years. Mary's brows were arched in question, and Tom's face looked like he was issuing a warning.

When their silent conversation finally stopped they both looked directly at me. Tom sighed deeply and looked apologetic as Mary began to speak.

"We've been trying to stay out of this, Lo, really, we have. But you're like a daughter to us, and Parker is our nephew."

Oh shit! This can't be good!

"We can't help but notice that something is…well I'm just going to come out with it. Something is going on between you two."

I shifted nervously in my chair trying to avoid eye contact. I could feel the hot pink shame rise up through my cheeks. Speechless, I grabbed my drink and downed it in one gulp. Although it wasn't a direct question, I knew she was waiting for some sort of explanation, and at this point I had nothing to offer.

What seemed like minutes passed, before Tom finally chimed in. "Lauren, we didn't mean to make you uncomfortable," he soothed, giving Mary an admonishing glance. "What Mary… I mean what *we* were trying to say is that we love you both, and whatever may or may not be going on is really none of our business. We just hope that whatever *it* is you two may finally acknowledge it now that you're older."

Mary looked like she was about to explode, and I knew I was in for a healthy dose of her motherly advice. I took a deep breath and gestured to our server for another drink while secretly wishing she would bring the entire bottle of Gray Goose back instead.

"Lauren, I see the way you look at each other. Tom and I still look at each other the same way after forty years of marriage!"

With a thin smile, Tom raised his eyebrows, half in agreement and half in apology for what we were about to endure.

"I've known since you were teenagers that there was a certain spark between you. It's something that just doesn't happen every day you know. It's very special, dear."

I listened quietly and tried to absorb it all as I glanced at the door hoping my drink, or my bottle, would arrive any second.

"I know you're engaged, and I know Parker's had his share of, well, companions, but I always knew in my heart that the two of you were destined to be together someday."

I couldn't move. Couldn't breathe. When Tara finally arrived with my martini, I dragged my eyes from the table to meet hers and managed to utter, "Keep 'em coming please." She must have thought I was crazy, but she nodded as though she understood before disappearing back through the tavern door.

Sensing my discomfort, Mary added, "Lauren, please don't be upset with us. We aren't trying to interfere with your life. I've just been so worried about my nephew lately, I thought that if he saw you again maybe he would..."

She was worried about Parker? Why? Why was she so concerned? Now she had my full attention. I needed to know the reason behind her mysterious worry, so I reluctantly joined the conversation.

"I love you, too, and I'm not upset with you, but I don't know why you would bring him here hoping that I might be able to help him after all these years. What do you want me to do? I guess I just don't understand."

Tom and Mary exchanged glances. Mary's eyes suddenly looked glassy, and she took a drink and cleared her throat. I studied her trying to figure out what was going on. Mary was always composed, laid back even. When Sarah and I were young she never even raised her voice when we got into trouble. Seeing her like this scared me.

Her voice cracked when she spoke, "Tell her, Tom."

I waited anxiously for an explanation as Tom put his arm around Mary before turning his attention to me. "Lo, we're concerned that Parker may never experience real love." Looking at the table he let out a long breath.

"After his father died a few years ago, he quit the family business and started playing professional poker. We supported his decision at first, I mean he's good. He's built his own fortune; traveled around the world, and we're quite proud of him really."

Mary wiped the tears that were now dripping down her cheeks and glanced at Tom before starting in again. "We always wondered why Parker never brought a date to any of our family gatherings. He's never even talked about having a girlfriend. He's been so distant since his dad died. For a minute we even thought he might be gay."

She fidgeted with her wedding ring and laughed nervously as though she were relieving the built up tension. "I was getting so worried about him, I started asking around. You know you can always dig up gossip in high society circles. It seems like every one of those old bags at the country club is on a mission to see who they can cover in the most mud. Anyway, I've heard rumors that Parker is living a very wild lifestyle. I don't even want to say this out loud," she lowered her voice to a whisper, "but they say he keeps company with high priced escorts, Lo."

I sank back in my chair in disbelief as the word "escorts" rang in my ears. *No! Parker Blackwell could easily have any woman he wanted. Why in the world would he spend time or money on prostitutes?*

"I know what you're thinking, Lo. I thought the same thing when I heard. Parker is much too handsome and too smart to do something like that, but it's true, and I've been worried sick ever since I found out. I'm so sorry to have to tell you these things about him. I'm sorry I brought him here like this. I didn't know you were engaged. I just had to see what would happen if you two were together again. I had to see if there was a chance…"

My heart ached as images of Parker rolling around in bed with prostitutes raced through my head. Suddenly,

Mary's voice seemed far away, almost like I was watching a scene from a movie. *This isn't happening.*

"If that wasn't bad enough," Mary continued, "Rumor has it that he recently signed with some ruthless agent who's exploiting his bad boy image to get him a deal with Rebel Spirits. Have you seen those awful liquor commercials where the men are draped in half-naked women?"

Tears were streaming down Mary's face, and my stomach was churning. I began to regret downing two martinis in the last fifteen minutes, or maybe I just wished it had been four. Hell, I wasn't sure at this point. I didn't know what to say, and I was already planning my escape. When my phone started ringing from inside my purse, I grasped the opportunity like a lifeline.

I looked at the two of them sitting across from me in despair, and almost changed my mind, but seeing them like that was more than I could bare. "I'm sorry, I'm going to have to take this," I said as I answered the call.

When I heard the sweet sound of Nina's voice on the other end I knew exactly what to do.

"Lo, sorry to interrupt. Steve said you were having dinner with the Blackwells, but I wanted to check on you since you haven't called. I saw Parker in the lobby earlier, and holy fuck, you're right about his..."

Trying to sound concerned, I cut her off in midsentence. "Absolutely, I'll be right there."

"What? What are you talking about?" I could hear Nina's confusion as I hung up the phone and turned to Mary and Tom. It hurt to look at them. Mary's nose was red, and her tears had left trails through the make-up on her cheeks. Tom was rubbing her back looking up at me as though I could offer something, anything to help them.

I hugged each of them quickly and excused myself. "I'm so sorry, but that was the front desk. There's a problem that I need to attend to right away." Leaving them like this made me sick, but it was the only thing I could do.

"I love you both so much. I know things with Parker will be just fine. I mean, he comes from a great family, right?" I bit my lip to fend off the tears. "Oh, and I had a really nice time with you this weekend. Please tell Sarah to call me." Before the last words left my lips I was already walking away.

Eight

YOU CAN RUN, BUT YOU CAN'T HIDE

I knew Nina was worried, but she's been my best friend since first grade, and I knew she'd understand once I had the chance to explain. Right now, I couldn't breathe. So much had happened in the last two days. I was so overwhelmed that my mind flipped the switch to autopilot as I passed through the tavern, across the lobby and out the back door in route to the one place where I could escape everything. When the fresh lake air kissed my face, I kicked off my shoes and kept walking until I felt wet sand between my toes at the water's edge. Then I ran.

When everything was spinning out of control, running kept me sane. It kept my demons from catching up, kept me from screaming at God, asking why me, and it kept me from harboring the kind of self-pity that whittles away at a person until she is nothing but an empty shell.

I started the week my mom died. I was walking on the beach trying to understand why my life was being ripped apart at the seams. With tears streaming down my face and my heartbeat pounding in my ears, I just kept walking faster and faster as if I could escape it all somehow. Finally, and without really knowing what I was doing, I started to run. I ran for what seemed like a mile in the sand until I couldn't run anymore, until my legs felt like rubber and I collapsed from the sheer exhaustion of spent energy and emotion. Aside from sex it was the best release I'd ever known. With the intimacy lacking between Jake and I lately, the minute I reached a nice brisk pace my body told me I was way overdo.

Emotion. Funny how one little word could hold so much weight. It could steer me like the current and alter my course like the wind. One minute I was going along steady and sure and the next I was being knocked off my feet by some unexpected emotion. In the past it was grief, sadness, even anger, but now? Now, I wasn't sure what I was feeling, and I don't know what's worse. Maybe something's been missing, and I never even realized it until now.

Have you ever lost something and then forgot all about it until you suddenly needed it again? *What did I need? What had I lost?*

My mind went back to Parker's words. "I take pleasure when I need it and give it when I choose. Sex and love are two different things…"

Pushing myself hard, I kept going until I reached the lighthouse and the brink of collapse. As I sat on the edge of the pier to catch my breath, something caught my eye. Parker was walking towards me. *What was he doing here?*

I leaned back and let the breeze cool me as I watched him move closer with confident strides. His unbuttoned shirt flapped in the wind, exposing his chiseled chest and stomach. The five o'clock shadow he'd developed over the weekend complimented his dazzling white smile that was visible from a mile away, and I wondered briefly why he had to be so fucking irresistible and aggravating all at the same time.

"I was on my way back from town when I saw you running down the beach. I had a feeling you'd end up here." His eyes sparkled in the sun as he spoke. He towered over me, and my anger began to melt away as I thought about how his mouth felt on my body.

"So, you've resorted to stalking me now?" My lips pressed together tightly, as I wondered how badly my make-up was smudged and smeared from the mixture of sweat and tears.

He laughed. "Remember how much time we spent out here, jumping off the pier, racing up the stairs in the lighthouse?"

"Yeah, I do. We had some great times." Staring down at the black boulders under the clear blue water below, I played back the many scenes, jumping off the pier in our bathing suits, racing to the buoy and back, and laughing until our stomachs hurt.

"Some of the best memories I had in my life included you, Lo, and I want to make more with that vibrant girl I used to know. I want to see you live again, you know? Feel the adrenaline pumping through your veins? When's the last time you let loose and did something crazy?"

I sat in awe of the boy I used to know and the beautiful flawed man he had become. I almost forgot how much I missed him; how much he meant to me. If anyone asked back then, I would've said I hated his guts, but inside I knew better. Inside I thought about him day and night. I wanted to win every challenge just so he would admire me, and every time we were close enough, I secretly wished he would kiss me and sometimes more…

I studied his face and thought about the pain he experienced in his life. He never had a stable home. All the money in the world couldn't replace something like that. The gleam in his eyes made it hard for me to stay mad, but after a few seconds passed without a reply he relented. The way he tilted his head to the side and flashed his dimples, I knew whatever he had to say was sure to be good.

"Okay, I'm sorry. I didn't mean to make you feel like a charity case or whatever you said earlier. The truth is I want to be your friend, and I still want to fuck your brains out," he looked out over the water, "Saving you from yourself is just the added bonus you'll receive should you choose to accept my generous offer."

Ahh, there's the arrogant bastard I know and love. I threw my head back laughing and punched him in the arm. "You always did have to be a smartass!" The release of emotions felt incredible. I was high on endorphins, his aura and something else. Pheromones. He seemed to notice.

"Are you trying to tell me you like it rough? Well, that could be arranged…" That sinfully seductive smile appeared, and I couldn't stop staring at him. Mesmerized, I was completely under his spell.

"That's my girl. I almost wondered if I'd lost my touch with you," he laughed. "Come on, let's go back to the tavern and have a few drinks for old time's sake. I'll be out of your hair in the morning, but until then, I need you to promise me one thing."

I was instantly curious. "What's that?"

"Promise me from this moment on you'll tell me if you need me--for anything, Lo."

When he held out his pinky, I sighed loudly and rolled my eyes. When we were kids we only saved the pinky swear for the most serious promises. The kind that could involve severe consequences if ever discovered.

"Wow! You must be serious if you're asking me to pinky swear!" I smirked and curled my pinky around his.

The moment our fingers hooked he pulled me toward him kissing me softly on the forehead. "Deadly serious."

The thought of him living such an empty life alone made my heart ache. I wished we could go back seven summers, and wondered if maybe things would've turned out differently. *If there was any way I could freeze time, I would do it now.* I thought, as I took his hand and followed him to his car.

"Parker?"

"Yeah?" He slid his arm comfortably around my shoulder as we walked together.

"I don't want to go to the tavern."

Parker turned to face me placing a hand on my shoulder while the other gently cupped my chin. He tilted my face to his gently, wiping my tear stained cheeks. "Where do you want to go, Lo? We can go anywhere. Just say the word. How about Vegas?"

My brow furrowed, but softened as I became lost in his deep sparkling emerald pools and dimples. Completely mesmerized by his charm for a moment, I almost forgot what I was going to say. *How does he do that to me?*

Then it registered. "Vegas?" I laughed, "I was thinking more like taking one last drive in that obscenely beautiful car of yours." My face almost ached from smiling at the thought of his spontaneous request. *I mean Vegas? Really? Did he honestly think that was an option?*

"So, let me get this straight," he said grinning from ear-to-ear. "I offer you a chance to go anywhere in the world, and I mean anywhere, and all you want to do is go for a ride in my car?" He shook his head, clearly amused as he reached down to brush a wisp of hair from my cheek.

Letting my mind wander for a minute, I thought about how it would feel to have the freedom to go anywhere on a whim. The offer was surprisingly tempting, but I knew my reality and his were worlds apart. The Grand was my reality, and it required my complete attention, especially now…and then there was Jake. A random thought popped in my head. *What happens in Vegas stays in Vegas.* I remembered the conversation with Tom and Mary and a shiver went down my spine. I looked at this man who could have anything in the world and wondered why he would deny himself love. *Love of all things?*

"Did I lose you?" His car door slammed jarring me to attention. He had opened my door and let me in the car, and I hadn't even noticed. *Snap out of it!*

"No, I'm here. Just daydreaming, I guess."

"Mmm…about what?" A hungry look came over his face, and he cocked his head waiting for my answer.

The way he changed gears so quickly made me giggle, and my insides began to melt. "Is your mind always in the gutter?" I shook my head.

"Honestly? Yeah, most of the time, but especially when I'm with you." Giving me a mischievous sideways glance he continued. "Maybe it has something to do with needing closure."

Nine

GIVING IN

His Mercedes roared to life, slamming me back in the seat as we pulled out onto the winding road that followed the shore. Just a few days ago, I never thought I'd see him again, now here I was sitting next to him after all these years. A strange mixture of emotions filled my heart. I knew I should feel guilty, after all, I was engaged. I was fully aware that sitting next to this tall, blonde, and dangerously-fuckable man I barely knew, was the last place on Earth I should be, but somehow it didn't matter. I didn't want to be anywhere else in the world but right here, right now. I could see the sign to Thompson's Store up ahead. When I noticed we were slowing down, I shot Parker a questioning look.

"What are you thinking about?" he said still looking straight ahead.

"The stars. I was thinking about the stars and how bright they are tonight." It wasn't a complete lie. I was looking at the stars even if I wasn't thinking about them.

"The stars, huh?" he chuckled. "Yeah, I haven't seen them like this in a long time. The lights in Vegas seem to drown them out. I have to go to the desert to really see them."

"Do you? Go to the desert I mean?"

"I have a few times. Maybe you could come with me?" He said as he wheeled into the parking lot. "Hey, I'm running in the store. Do you want anything?"

"No, I'm good, but I'm coming in, too. I have to use the ladies' room."

Parker held the door open, and I went directly to the restroom in the back. When we were kids we'd ride our bikes to this place almost daily for candy and slushes. I still stop by a couple times a month for some chocolate to help fuel my late work nights. I didn't see who was working the counter tonight, but I wondered briefly if Old Man Thompson would remember Parker.

When I exited the bathroom, a squeal of high pitched laughter rang out from the front of the store. My eyes narrowed as I made my way up to the counter, where I saw the Thompsons' oldest daughter, Lisa, leaning over staring up at Parker with stars in her eyes. She couldn't be more than nineteen, but her outfit made her look like she worked at a strip club rather than a convenience store. I cleared my throat and took my place next to him, eyeing her suspiciously.

"Oh, hi, Lo! I can't believe you know Parker Blackwell! I watch him on TV every chance I get. I just can't even believe he's like standing right here in person!"

Her sugary sweet tone gushed over me, and I noticed her eyes soaking in every inch of him.

I scowled, and Parker shrugged at me with a stupid, boyish grin that somehow managed to soften my lips into a smile. I knew he couldn't help it. He had a powerful effect on women.

"Yep, he's something isn't he?" I rolled my eyes and headed for the door. "You should get his autograph, Lisa."

"Oh, good idea," she squealed as I pushed the door open and headed back to the car.

A few seconds later Parker appeared shaking his head and smiling. "Thanks a lot," he said as he slid into the driver's seat.

I blinked at him innocently. "For what? You must be used to women throwing themselves at your feet by now, huh?"

He titled his head inquisitively. "If I didn't know any better, Lauren St. John, I'd say you're jealous."

"You wish!" I snapped back suddenly noticing the brown paper sack he was holding. "So, what's in the bag?"

"Ha, wouldn't you like to know?" He laughed playfully and clutched the bag tightly against him. "I'll give you one guess then I'll let you resort to offering sexual favors for clues."

I burst out laughing, and he reached over and tickled me until I couldn't catch my breath.

"Stop!" I squealed, helplessly struggling against the seatbelt to escape. I arched my back and his fingers inadvertently brushed over my breast silencing me instantly. His hand lingered briefly, and he caught my hardened nipple between his finger and thumb causing me to moan. Liquid heat rushed lower. There was a brief silence in the air before he removed his hand and I heard the bag rustle.

Wishing he hadn't stopped, I was pouting as I turned to face him and watched him slowly remove a bottle of strawberry wine from the bag. The last summer he visited we had my older cousin buy us a few bottles, and we finished them off on the beach one night while playing truth or dare. *He remembered.*

His gaze was intent as he awaited my reaction. "You're still ticklish I see. Do you know what I want to do to that mouth when you pout like that?" His voice was thick and warm, igniting little fires across my skin.

"What do you want to do to my mouth?" I dared him to answer.

His dimples made an appearance causing me to blush as we both imagined the possibilities. He started the car and threw it in gear. I leaned back into the seat focusing on the stars to regain my composure. A few minutes later, he pulled the car into the parking lot near the pier.

He turned off the engine. "It's a nice night for a walk on the beach, don't you think?"

"I'm game." I could barely calm the nervous fluttering in my stomach as I thought about what was about to happen. Parker grabbed a blanket from the trunk, slung it over his shoulder, and handed me a bottle of wine. We walked down the shore for a while hand in hand, taking swigs from our bottles and laughing at the crazy things we tried to get away with those nights after the adults had a couple of drinks under their belts.

When we reached a secluded section of beach far from the parking lot, Parker spread the blanket out on the sand and motioned for me to sit next to him. Adrenaline coursed through my body as his arm circled my waist. I leaned against his shoulder absorbing his intoxicating smell and the heat of his skin against mine. His fingers brushed seductively along my collar bone then dipped just below the front of my dress. My breath hitched. I tensed as I felt my nipples harden in response, and my gaze, full of desire, connected with his.

The moonlight captured his tongue flicking over his bottom lip. The deep green pools of his eyes were heavy with desire, yet they still seemed to knowingly penetrate mine. I let out a small scream when he laid back on the blanket without warning, pulling me with him so I straddled his lap. His hands went to the hem of my dress lifting it slowly, and I raised my arms allowing him to remove it and toss it aside. All the while, I felt his eyes burning a trail down my body, greedily devouring every inch of exposed skin. I reached for the button of his pants, but he brushed my hands away and trailed his fingertips lightly up my sides stopping to caress my breasts. I dropped my head back, placing my hands on his thighs and pressed my hot core into his hard length beneath me, letting him know I was ready to take all that he could offer.

Inhaling sharply, he pulled me down into his kiss, sending tingles of desire through my entire system as his mouth ravaged mine. I rocked against him, my passion saturating through my panties. I wanted to remove the last barriers between us, and I reached for his pants again. Cooperating this time, he helped me pull them down along with his boxers until the full measure of his hard cock sprung free. I admired it blatantly as he took a condom from his wallet and rolled it down over his length. My tongue swirled over my lips instinctively at the thought of taking his swollen member between my lips. Sensing my intentions, he captured my wrists in his hand and rolled me on my back.

His voice came husky and low in my ear. "Ladies first," he growled before lowering his head to lick and suck my breasts. He ripped my panties down as his skillful tongue worked me into a frenzy, and I squirmed and bucked into him while his mouth created intense sensations that connected directly to my core.

He lowered his head to work his way down my body, but I protested. It felt like we'd waited a lifetime for this moment, and I needed him now. I ground my hips against him, my clit desperately seeking the delicious friction the broad smooth head of his cock could provide.

His eyelids were heavy with desire as he pulled back for a brief moment with his tip pressed solidly against my entrance. His body froze as I thrust my hips up begging for him to enter me.

"Not yet." His eyes squeezed shut, and he let out a loud groan of resistance before pinning my thighs with his hands. "I want all of you," he said as he dipped his head and began licking a path down my stomach. I thrust my hands in his hair as he nipped and sucked his way down spreading my legs roughly when he reached his destination.

My body stiffened and arched as his tongue dipped into my saturated folds. He licked attentively, bathing his tongue in my wetness before swirling it around my swollen clit. I gasped, and pulled at his hair, at the sensation of two thick fingers pressing into me slowly. Placing his mouth fully over my clit he increased the pressure and began thrusting his fingers into me deeper and faster. The pleasure building inside forced me toward the edge until my mind went blank. I called out his name through a ragged breath as the waves consumed me and exploded in tiny white sparks.

He pulled his fingers from me and placed them in his mouth licking them clean of my essence. The primal act shocked me and instantly made me ache for more. He slid up my body and kissed me roughly brushing his chest over my breasts, and my body trembled with a mixture of pleasure and pain as he slowly sank every inch of his rigid

cock deep into my wetness. I held my breath as his thrusts

filled me with delicious pressure. His growls came through

gritted teeth as he moved deliberately in and out, stretching

me. I moved my hips to take all of him as his girth

pleasured the spot deep within. Sensing I was close, his

pace increased. I felt his member swell, as he pummeled

into me faster.

"Parker!" I cried out as my body unraveled with wave

after wave contracting around him. He groaned loudly and

his body stiffened as he thrust himself forcefully into me

one last time.

Minutes passed as we lay together under the stars and

listened to the waves lapping on the shore. Finally, he

nuzzled his face against my chest and drew out of me

slowly.

"Lo," he whispered as he cupped my face gently, "Are you okay?"

I bit my lip, considering my answer carefully. I wasn't okay. In fact, I was far from okay. This night had changed everything, and I knew I could never go back. A lump formed in my throat and panic and guilt washed over me at the thought of choosing between Parker and Jake, but I couldn't let him know what I was feeling. I didn't want him to think this was a mistake.

Sitting upright and taking a long drink of wine, I decided to make a joke to lighten the mood. "I'm fine," I said calmly flashing a smile. "If you were trying to hurt me you'll have to try a whole lot harder next time." *Next time? I couldn't believe my own ears. Why did I say that?*

He was silent. Just as I started to wonder if I'd hurt his feelings he smiled and tackled me to the ground holding my arms at my sides. "Next time? Is that a challenge? If so I could hurt you right now." He lowered his head and nipped roughly at the undersides of my breasts.

My heart pounded in my chest as I strained against him, and although just minutes before he had satisfied me more than any man I'd ever been with, liquid desire already pooled between my legs. I groaned and shifted beneath him absorbing the pleasure as he sucked each nipple thoroughly.

Suddenly, he stopped and laid his head against my chest. I opened my eyes, confused at his reaction and pushed against him, sitting up to look at his face. "What's wrong?"

He let out a sigh, his face full of disappointment. "I only had one condom."

I laughed and pushed him onto his back. With a raised brow I whispered seductively, "Good thing I'm on the pill." An instant look of relief washed over his face, and I felt him relax as he tipped his head back and closed his eyes. I began kissing and licking a trail over the hard muscles of his belly. His thick member was fully engorged by the time my tongue reached the tip and flicked over it lightly causing his breathing to quicken as I licked down to the base and back up swirling my tongue and sucking along his full length. I wrapped my fingers around him feeling his full weight in my hand then took the head between my lips. His body flinched, and I moaned at his reaction before clamping my mouth around him and taking his cock all the way to the back of my throat. His hand twisted in my hair, and he growled my name encouraging my need to pleasure him even more. I withdrew slowly, holding just the head in my mouth and sucking before taking him all the way down in long slow strokes. I moved faster cupping his balls in my hand until I felt them tighten, his cock twitching in my mouth. He tightened his grip on my hair, holding me still before relaxing again when the sensation passed. I looked up at him begging for permission to continue.

"I want to be inside you, Lo."

I wanted him, too. I wanted to feel him inside me with nothing in between. I crawled up to straddle him, grabbing his cock firmly and rubbing it across my wet slit. His hands squeezed my thighs as I pleasured my clit with his length until I ached for him to fill me. Easing down onto him until I sheathed him completely in my wetness, I stopped. The sensation was almost too much to bare. He reached up and squeezed my nipples, spurring me to ride him hard until my orgasm ripped through me. My entire body convulsed as his thrusts matched mine long after the last wave subsided.

I sat still holding him deep inside of me then leaned my head back and braced my hands against his chest. As I closed my eyes he reminded me that he was going to win this challenge.

"Mmm. Not so fast. You dared me to hurt you, remember?" He thrust slowly into me. "If you changed your mind you better tell me now, because I fully intend to."

My eyes snapped open to meet his. The look on his face told me he wasn't done with me yet, and my pulse quickened as my body began to respond to his once again. He lifted me gently and got behind me clasping both wrists in his hand and grabbing my chin firmly with the other before whispering in my ear.

The scruff of his jaw scratched my neck as he spoke. "I'm going to hurt you now, Lo. Is that what you want?" he growled, his hard length pressing roughly against my back.

A mixture of fear and adrenaline coursed through me as the opening of my sex clenched in anticipation. I nodded slowly, and he pushed my face down into the blanket forcing my thighs apart with his. I braced myself for him, and his first thrust sent me reeling. Pain seared into me, and I screamed as he slammed into me relentlessly. My nipples, already sensitive from his mouth, throbbed from the friction of the blanket beneath me. I bit my lip, and my mind went blank as the pain began to subside and somewhere outside myself I heard my own voice screaming out.

"Yes! Fuck yes! Fuck me harder!" My backside slammed against him thrust for thrust as the orgasm rocked my body and squeezed around his cock until I felt him spasm, filling me completely with spurts of his warm, soothing fluid.

His heart was pounding in his chest when he lifted me back against him. His arms circled my stomach, and he rubbed his face in my hair. When I tried to move he held me tight.

"Tell me now that we weren't meant to be together."

My voice was barely a whisper. "Parker, I..." I couldn't deny it. The emotions, the pleasure that he gave me...it was overwhelming. Every part of me wanted him, wanted everything about him. Tears welled up in my eyes, and I had to squeeze them shut tightly before they spilled over and opened the flood gates that I fought so hard to keep closed.

"Shh, you don't have to say anything. I already know the answer. I'm the right man for you, Lo. I always have been. I know you don't see it now, but you will soon enough."

Ten

REVELATIONS

"Lo, what in the hell are you doing out here?" The sound of Jake's voice jarred me awake, and I peeled my face from the patio chair to blink up at him and absorb my surroundings. It was sunrise.

"I don't know. I must have fallen asleep," I stuttered looking around, "I had some wine and…"

He ran his hand through his hair then gripped the railing of the balcony as he looked out at the beach with his lips pressed together in a thin white line. *What the hell was HE doing out here?*

I scrambled to gather my thoughts. *Damn it, Lo! How could you fall asleep with the scent of Parker all over you?* Panic set in as I began to recall what happened just a few hours before. Parker walked me to my suite. I remembered feeling emotionally and physically exhausted and sitting in the chair on the balcony for a minute listening to the sound of the waves and…

I breathed a sigh of relief when Jake turned and walked into my suite closing the door behind him. Grateful to have a moment to gather my thoughts, I closed my eyes as I sank back into the chair. Jake was never one for conflict, and right now I was thankful, but lately when I needed him most he would just shut down. At times his silence hurt worse than any words he could possibly say.

A confusing mixture of guilt and anger swept over me as I thought about how we'd grown apart. I tried to justify things in my mind—financial stress, our demanding jobs, but things between us had been tense for almost a year now. The more I focused on The Grand, the more distant Jake became. He spent more time at work, even taking jobs out-of-town. I'd grown bitter over his lack of support, and sometimes my moods switched between loving him and hating him in a matter of days. There were times I wondered why we were even considering marriage, and after last night I was questioning it more than ever.

The thought made me panic. Jake and The Grand were the only two things I could count on in my life, besides Nina. Jake was there for me when my father remarried, and the day I got the shattering news that he had a heart attack at work. He was by my side through the funeral and all the days after when I could barely manage to drag myself out of bed. We loved each other, and back then I was sure he was the man I wanted to marry someday. So why did it suddenly feel like everything was changing?

Maybe we were just going through a rough spell. All couples go through them at one point or another. And what happened with Parker--as much as I wanted to call it a mistake, I couldn't. It was closure. Nothing more nothing less. I needed to close the door on The Parker Chapter in my life in order to move on, and in a few short hours he would be hundreds of miles away, and everything would be back to normal.

I tried to convince myself, but deep inside I had a nagging feeling that somehow things would never be the same. Our relationship had been unraveling slowly, long before seeing Parker again, so why was it so hard to admit? Could my fear of being alone be keeping me from facing the truth? Maybe Jake and I no longer wanted the same things.

I blinked back tears as the red warmth of the sun shined through my eyelids. The thought of facing Jake made my head pound harder, and my entire body throbbed like I had been run over by a truck. It would take every bit of energy to peel myself from the chair. *And then what? Should I confess and beg for forgiveness?* My heart pounded until adrenaline finally forced me to my feet. I didn't know what to say, but there was one thing I was sure of. I wanted to get this over with as quickly as possible.

I froze the moment I slid the door open, and my breath hitched at the sight of him leaned over the counter with his head in his hands, waiting.

"Lo, what the hell is wrong with you? You've been drinking too much; hardly sleeping. I don't even remember the last time we had sex…" his voice trailed off. *Sex! Ugh! Why did he have to bring that up?*

Thankful he didn't push for details about last night, I quickly followed his lead. "I know," I replied, trying to keep my voice from betraying my anxiety level. "I'm working on it, Jake. I'm trying some new ideas, and things are starting to turn around. Once I get The Grandview back on track we can focus on us again. You'll see."

He gave me a look as if to say "I don't believe you" then hesitated like he was struggling to hold back the rest of his thoughts. I stood crossing my arms in a silent shield that willed him to keep his distance, then breathed a sigh of relief when he turned toward the door without looking back.

"I came home to grab some clean clothes. Looks like I'll be staying on the job until sometime next week." Holding the door halfway open his back still to me he paused. "But whatever is going on between us can't wait that long. We need to talk tonight, Lauren. I'll call you around nine."

Did he just call me 'Lauren'? Oh, he must be really mad.

I wanted to say something, anything to relieve the tension between us, but I hesitated too long, and the door closed behind him before I could find the words.

I shuffled to the bathroom of the little suite I called home since Evelyn came along. Thankful it was Sunday morning and most of the guests would be checking out by the time I was ready to go downstairs, I took my time knowing I could get to my office relatively unnoticed.

I was completely exhausted as I stepped into the shower and felt the tension instantly begin to melt. Some of my best thinking was done in the shower, and I needed a game plan now more than ever. I wasn't about to let The Grand lose her newly found momentum, and as much as I wanted to avoid it, I needed to resolve things with Jake.

I lost my head this weekend. No, I completely lost my fucking mind. With The Grand hanging in the balance and my relationship with Jake already strained, seeing Parker again was enough to send me over the edge. But that was over now, and I had to leave it in the past with all the other memories of him. Whatever happened, whatever I felt, couldn't be real. The chemistry was undeniable, explosive even, but I didn't know if I could ever fully trust Parker. *Auras.* Nina was right. Jake was my real, but I shut him out. I shut him out then betrayed him. Why? Because while I was trying to hold on to the only life I'd ever known, I neglected the only person I imagined sharing it with. My life was here at The Grandview, and living it without Jake was... my stomach clenched at the thought.

Jake was right, too. I had become distant, drinking more than usual, working late. The breakdown in our relationship was mostly on me. *Why did I let it get this far?* I had to make things right. Starting with the phone call tonight.

My head throbbed with dread, but I had to change things, and I would. Cutting down on the drinking would be easy, but using my time more productively so my nights could be free to spend with him might be a problem. I'd thought about hiring an assistant for some time, but with money so tight it wasn't an option right now. Maybe I could check with the local college about the possibility of offering an unpaid internship.

As long as Jake never found out about this weekend we still had a chance. How could I be so stupid? I needed him. I needed him to love me, and to be invested in the future of The Grandview again. I desperately needed the loving compassionate man he used to be. The one who held me when I cried, picked me flowers on the side of the road and serenaded me with every song on the radio when we took our long Sunday drives up the coast. Did he still love me, or had things between us changed that much? An unnerving thought entered my mind. *If I loved him then how could I have shared myself with Parker without a second thought?*

I couldn't let myself go down that road. Not now. I had to stay focused on the present and the things that were real.

Parker was unfinished business until last night. Now it was time to move on. Besides, I was sure he'd have no trouble doing just that. He probably had a list of women who'd be more than happy to keep his bed warm every night. A wave of nausea swept over me. *I'm not jealous!* I screamed at myself. Parker Blackwell could do whatever he damn well pleased. I was just thankful he'd be doing it far away in Las Vegas.

My throbbing head reminded me I needed coffee and a plan. I knew how I would deal with Jake, now I had to put some plans in motion for The Grand. I would ask Nina to call a staff meeting for tomorrow morning. We had to keep every penny from rolling out the door, and I would need help to determine where we could make some cuts.

Now where was my cell phone? Looking around I spotted it blinking on the nightstand. It was a missed call from Barry Stanton, dad's attorney and old family friend.

My knees felt weak as I sat on the bed to listen. Hearing from Barry on a Sunday couldn't be good.

"Lauren, this is Barry. I know it's Sunday, but could you come down to my office this afternoon to discuss the situation with The Grandview? Evelyn's attorney called to give me a heads up..." he paused, "She wants to sell her shares, and you'll have ninety days to come up with the money. The clock starts ticking tomorrow. I hope to see you around two."

I was reeling. I felt like I'd been punched in the gut, and everything inside me was being abruptly ejected. Dropping the phone on the bed I ran to the bathroom and barely made it in the door when the liquid contents of my stomach discharged, splattering explosively across the tile. Dropping to my knees, I braced myself against the toilet until the violent contractions stopped, and tears stung my eyes as I slumped there unable to move. One thought kept replaying in my mind. *That greedy, fucking bitch!*

Things hadn't been the same since the day she slithered into our lives. I hated her, and I never forgave my dad for marrying her. She closed in on him like a wounded animal. While half of him wanted to run away, the other half was in desperate need of care, and he fell prey to her devious tactics. Until then I had everything, an amazing family, The Grandview, and Jake.

Now my parents were gone, my relationship with Jake was rocky, and the family business that I loved my entire life could be ripped away. I didn't have time to feel sorry for myself. I had to think fast, and I had to see Nina right away.

Eleven

THE PIMP WORE PRADA

Ten minutes later I pulled myself together and was clicking down the hall in my black sling-back pumps. I did the best I could to thank a few departing guests as I made my way to the kitchen aware that my gurgling stomach could unleash again at any moment. Waves of nausea rippled through me as I followed the invisible trail of aromas through the swinging doors.

The smell, especially in the morning, was usually one of my favorite things about The Grand. Everything about her felt like home--everything. Morning sunlight filled her to the brim bouncing across the maple floors. On summer nights flames from the bonfire danced and reflected across tinkling glasses filled with summer's most intoxicating concoctions. There was live music and laughter, and smiling guests danced, sang and enjoyed to excess. In these walls lived an unmistakable feeling that everything was right in the world. Until now.

In the kitchen the full force of sausage, eggs and bacon filled the air and I fought to keep my composure as I scanned the room for Nina, but even in this state of despair I felt lucky. I had lived my whole life on vacation. People who came to The Grandview were only visiting for a short time. I got to see them at their happiest, full of kindness, enjoying the finest food, wine, the white sandy beaches and the most luxurious cotton sheets. All the while cameras were clicking capturing each joyous scene. Until now, it never occurred to me that there was anything other than life at The Grandview. Being on vacation every day was the only life I'd ever known, and I wasn't about to let anyone change that. Not Evelyn. Not anyone.

Things were bustling in the kitchen. Nina walked in just as I was about to give up, and she noticed immediately that something was desperately wrong.

She smiled thinly. "Hey, you okay?"

"No. I need to talk to you in my office," I whispered. "I'll grab you a coffee."

As Nina filled a plate, I grabbed a mug and stirred in two creams and two sugars, exactly how she liked it.

Moments later, I sat behind my desk with my head in my hands waiting for her. "Shut the door," I told her as she walked in already enjoying her breakfast. "Barry called this morning, and I have good news and bad news."

"Bad news first," she mumbled, covering her stuffed mouth as she spoke.

"Nina, this can't leave my office. You have to pinky swear."

"Are you fucking serious, Lo? Just tell me the bad news already."

"Not until you pinky swear." I understood why she was annoyed with my antics. So much was hanging in the balance, and here I was asking her to do something we did when we were about to confess which boy we were in love with each summer, but it didn't matter. Something about the gesture reassured me, like when Parker forced me to do it. I stuck out my pinky to show her I meant business.

Relenting, she rolled her eyes and wrapped her pinky finger around mine. "There. Now, please, this is obviously serious. You look like hell."

I scowled at her sarcastically. "Yes, it's very serious. That's why you had to pinky swear. What I'm about to tell you is crazy serious. It's so serious that I'm at a loss for what to do, and you know that doesn't happen to me very often."

"Fuck! Just say it already!"

"The Grandview is in trouble, Nina. Profits are down, and I found out this morning that my lovely business partner wants to sell her share. I have ninety days to come up with the money or it will go on the market."

Nina dropped her fork to her plate. She was silent, but the look on her face said it all. *That's right, Nina. Connect the dots. The huge mansion on the lake, the new forty foot boat docked at the marina, the Cadillac parked in the driveway. Evelyn had burned through all of my dad's money, and now she wanted to cash in on the one thing she had left.*

I waited for the enormity of my news to sink in. The color drained from her face. She cleared her throat and finally replied, "And there's good news?"

"Yes, the good news is that I only need to come up with twenty-five percent to pay her off, and with tourism and property values down, I'm hoping it'll be a number I can manage."

"What the fuck was your dad thinking leaving her ownership in The Grandview? What are you going to do Lo? That fucking bitch! I knew she was evil from the get go!"

Ah, organic girl at her best. Funny how such foul language could spew from my petite, peace-loving, save-the-world best friend. God, I loved her!

Her anger told me she was ready to go to battle, but what she did next confirmed it. Some people roll up their sleeves when they're ready to take care of business. Not Nina. The moment she set her glasses on my desk and gathered her hair in a bun at the back of her neck, I knew she was totally onboard.

"Yes, she's evil. This feels like the final blow, Nina. It will be final, too if I don't figure out a way to come up with the money."

"What do you mean come up with the money, Lo? Even at twenty-five percent, how could you possibly come up with that much in three months? Do you have some secret life I don't know about? Don't tell me you're auditioning for the next episode of *Locked up Abroad* or something?"

"This is clearly why we've been best friends for so long, Nina. Even when the chips are down your sense of humor doesn't miss a beat."

"Seriously, Lo. We need to do something about your chakras!" Her eyes narrowed as she waited for my response.

"I don't know yet, but I'm working on it. The chakras will have to wait for now. In the meantime, I need you to call a staff meeting for tomorrow morning. All the department heads should be there, kitchen manager, entertainment manager, housekeeping manager--everyone. I need to tell them myself and let them know that *I will* find the money no matter what it takes. I'm going to see Barry right now."

We were both thinking the same thing, but it was Nina who said it out loud. "Lo, I hate to say this but three months may not be long enough. There's a chance you…"

"I know what you're thinking, Nina, but losing this place isn't an option. I'll sell my fucking soul to the devil before I'll see my parents dream sold to the highest bidder."

"I know you will. That's what scares me. Please promise me you won't do anything crazy. I'm worried about you."

"I won't," I mumbled with a halfhearted smile. *Damn! She could always see right through me.*

"Pinky promise?"

I knew I couldn't. Instead I turned to her and rolled my eyes mockingly, "Are you fucking serious, Nina?"

Fifteen minutes later, I slammed on the brakes in front of Barry's office. My feet hit the pavement before I could rip the keys completely out of the ignition. I was on a mission. The receptionist's eyes were wide as I exploded through the door, and I heard her voice over my shoulder as I continued down the hall to Barry's office. *Barry's receptionist works on Sundays? Business must be good.*

"Hello, Miss St. John. Mr. Stanton is..." Mr. Stanton, please! He's been Barry since I was ten!

The door was open. "Hello, my dear!" Barry barked in the same booming tone that I'd always remembered.

"I'm sorry, Barry, I couldn't wait until two." We exchanged a quick hug, and he motioned for me to sit in the chair across from him as he walked back around his desk in shiny designer shoes.

"No problem. I have a few minutes. Can I get you anything, Lauren?" As he spoke, he nonchalantly smoothed down the graying hairs at his temples.

"Yeah, how about some fucking good news for a change? If one more thing goes wrong right now I think I might lose it!"

"Well, in that case, I think I can help. However, what we discuss here must stay within these four walls. Do you understand?"

Oh fuck! This feels like deja vu. Is he going to ask me to fucking pinky swear? "Of course, Barry, I understand. So what is it?"

He pulled a small box from the top drawer of his desk. "Your dad put this in a safety deposit box in my name when your mom passed away. It was part of her life insurance payment. He asked me to give it to you when you needed it most. That was the last smart thing that son-of-a-bitch did before he married that wretched stepmother of yours."

"Rest assured, she's nothing *of mine,* Barry. So what's in the box?"

"It's fifty thousand in cash, Lauren. It's not enough to bail you out all the way, but it's a step in the right direction."

Hot tears stung my eyes. I couldn't swallow. I could only stare at the box. My dad did care about my future in some way. At least he had enough sense to put something away for me. I knew I had to pull myself together before I ended up on Barry's floor sobbing my heart out. I was relieved when the sound of his voice brought me back to the moment.

"Lauren, he loved you very much. He just wasn't the same after your mom…" he stopped. The way I was glaring at him, he must have sensed my anger. I couldn't let myself go there. The only thing that mattered now was saving The Grandview.

"Yeah, I know, Barry. Thanks," I said, hoping to put an end to the topic. I felt like I should say something about my dad, something nice, but I refused to let myself think about him any longer.

"Lauren, there's something else I wanted to talk to you about. An opportunity."

Opportunity? Like I'm in any position for a fucking opportunity! "Barry, I really don't think I'm up for…"

He interrupted quickly, insisting I hear him out. "Lauren, do you know how you're going to come up with three hundred thousand dollars by September? If not I think you should listen to me."

Did he just say three hundred thousand! The nausea returned, and as a precaution I grabbed the small trash can from beside the desk. I didn't appreciate the stern tone in his voice, but I had to admit he was right. I had no idea where I would find that kind of money in three short months.

"To be honest, that's more than I thought it would be, and I don't have a plan yet, but I'm working on one. What are you offering?"

Studying my pale face, his voice softened. "It's a way for you to get out of this mess, but remember this can never leave this office. I'm trusting that you're an intelligent young woman. You've always been a free spirit, Lauren-- open-minded, too. That's why I agreed to this, well that and the fact that you need to make some serious cash very quickly."

Fucking spit it out already, Barry. What the fuck are you talking about? Are you involved in some kind of pyramid scam? Drug smuggling? Fuck! Dad always said you kept one foot on each side of the fence.

"If you're suggesting that I could make three hundred thousand in three months or less then you've definitely got my attention. So what's the offer?"

"That's my girl! I knew you would fight for what's yours, Lauren. You've always been a fighter. I think you would be willing to do whatever it takes to keep The Grandview wouldn't you?"

Nina's words from earlier flashed in my head. "Yes, I'm willing to fight, but what exactly are you talking about? This won't land me on an episode of *Locked Up Abroad* will it?" Suddenly her premonition didn't seem so unrealistic.

Barry let out a hearty laugh and slapped the desk hard as though it were the funniest thing he'd heard all day. The laughter eased him a little, but I hugged the trash can tighter, sensing that whatever he was about to tell me was difficult for him.

"Oh, Lauren, you're a feisty one. I assure you what I'm offering is completely legal. I'm an attorney after all. So here it is. I'm involved in another shall we say… enterprise, one that I conduct from my Las Vegas office. Let's call it a very lucrative hobby that employs beautiful women, very much like yourself. They travel to different cities, all expenses paid of course, and accompany very prominent successful men to events, on vacations…"

His voice faded as my mind began to process the enormity of his proposal. I was in shock. My ears were ringing, and my skin was on fire. *Did my dad's long-time friend, my trusted attorney just offer me a job as a call girl? This can't be happening!*

I jolted from the chair, halting him in mid-sentence. "Lauren, stop! Lauren, please hear me out!" He jumped up quickly and positioned himself against the door.

"Get the fuck out of my way, Barry!"

"Lauren, trust me. There's nothing illegal about this. My girls travel in private jets. They enjoy five star accommodations, world-class cuisine. They're treated like royalty in every way, Lauren, and I know what you're thinking. My clients don't pay for sex. They pay for companionship. Sex is optional and only if both parties agree to it."

My eyes bored holes straight through him as he tried to convince me, blurting out "the perks" in rapid fire succession. Never in my life had I wanted to physically aggress someone so badly.

"I'm done here!" I yelled at a volume I was sure the receptionist and any pedestrians on the sidewalk could hear. I was ready to remove Barry Stanton with my own two hands if I had to, and he sensed it as he cracked the door open slowly never taking his eyes off me.

Before he moved, he whispered one last thing, "Parker Blackwell, one of my best clients, requested you."

Hearing Parker's name in the midst of this nightmare was the final straw. I froze, my whole body shaking from the impact. *Fucking bastards! Both of you!* Barry finally stepped aside, and I stormed out.

"Have a good day, Miss St. John!" the receptionist called as I ran past the desk and out to the open air of the sidewalk. *Breathe!*

I felt for the side of the building to steady myself and looked out at the lake over the horizon. I stood there and stared, taking it all in for a moment when I remembered – *the money!* I left my money on that bastard's desk. I didn't want to go back, but I had no choice. *Fuck!*

As I turned around, Barry was standing at the door smugly extending the box in his hand. "I think you forgot something."

As I reached for the box, he leaned in and whispered, "He just wants to spend time with you, Lauren. He said you won't accept a loan, and he's willing to pay the three hundred thousand dollars for five days with you in Vegas." I ripped the box from his hands, and heard him call out one final time, "I'll need your answer by noon tomorrow."

Twelve

THE ULTIMATUM

Pretentious bastard! What the fuck was wrong with him! "Lucrative hobby!" "My girls!" Sick! He was sick! I always knew he was shady, but prostitution? He was a dirty old man. A pimp. How dare he think that I would consider prostitution! Had he no loyalty to my father at all? And what about Jake? Oh, he would put Barry's lights out when he found out about this!

Then there was Parker. Was this what he planned at his mysterious appointment with an unnamed attorney yesterday? Was he arranging another escort when Barry happened to tell him about The Grand, or did he go to Barry for information? He seemed to know something more than what he revealed. Did he think he could pay for me like one of his hired escorts? My head was spinning with questions. Did any of it even matter? The bottom line was unless I came up with the money I would lose The Grand for good, and Parker knew it. He knew it, and he was using it to manipulate me.

I pulled into the parking lot of The Grandview and took the back stairs to my suite to avoid being seen. Feeling scared and confused, all I could think about was talking to Jake, and soon. I had to collect myself. But how? Everything was falling apart, and I was running out of options. There's got to be something I can do to stop Evelyn, but three hundred thousand dollars was more money than I earned in three years let alone three months. Yet in my mind it didn't matter if it was thousands or millions, I knew I would do whatever it took to save my parents' dream and my only home from being ripped out from under me. I had to figure it out, but I had to be able to look at myself in the mirror afterwards.

Safely inside, I leaned against the door exhaling deeply, and for the first time I looked forward to the phone call with Jake. My mind kept repeating every horrible detail of my day--the confrontation, Evelyn wanting to sell The Grandview, the money my father left me, Barry's indecent proposal.

Anger and resentment filled my chest as the full impact of Parker's twisted offer hit me. It was pure extortion, but how much of it could I safely share with Jake without the whole thing exploding in my face?

My mind wouldn't stop racing, and I needed to feel Jake's arms around me. When things were hard in the past he was my rock. He wasn't big on words, but he always knew just what to do to make me feel safe, and I needed him more than ever.

Just then I caught a glimpse of my phone on the floor. I was so upset earlier that I'd left it behind. My heart dropped to my stomach as I looked at the screen. Two missed calls from Jake and a text message.

"Lo, where are you? I'm on my way home. I need to see you. This is too important to discuss on the phone."

I was panicked and relieved at the same time. I had to tell him as much as I could. Hell, I wanted to rip my heart open, spill it at his feet and beg for forgiveness, but I knew it would be a mistake. Knowing what I did would kill him. Tears stung my eyes as I realized what a mess I'd made. I needed to show Jake how much I loved him. I needed to make things right between us. Tonight could be a new beginning, and I wouldn't take any chances. Everything had to be just right.

As I stepped into the shower, I wondered if he'd want to make love to me after our heart-to-heart. My body needed him. I needed to erase the impression of Parker, and I had a feeling that Jake needed me, too. I longed to feel his love, and he longed for the sexual release that I'd denied him for far too long. Tonight we could both get everything we needed from each other, I thought as I dabbed my favorite perfume on my wrists and neck.

I examined my hair in the mirror and began applying lip gloss when I heard the door open. It had been too long since I'd made love to my future husband. I thought my body would start to react at the thought, but instead I felt nothing. Instead I was completely consumed with a mixture of panic and fear.

"Lo!" he called. I heard his keys drop onto the table by the door.

"In here!"

When he walked into the room I was posed seductively on the bed, my tan legs to one side. I could feel my nipples poking through my dress, and the look in his eyes told me he wanted me. Feeling relieved, I was ready for him to take me quickly, hoping I'd feel better when we were done, but something stopped him. He looked away, and I knew things were about to get intense.

"We need to talk, Lauren." The mood instantly changed.

"Let's talk later" I teased, pulling him down on the bed next to me and straddling his lap. He didn't look up to kiss me. He didn't pull my body close like I wanted him to. Instead he sat up with his arms at his sides and dropped his gaze to the floor.

I slid off his lap and sat quietly next to him, studying his face. "What's wrong, Jake? What happened?"

"It's what's *happening,* that I'm worried about."

"What do you mean? With The Grandview? "

"Yes, all of it. The drinking, the working late. It's put distance between us. You haven't been yourself for months. You've been so focused on keeping this place afloat and keeping Evelyn happy that you don't even see you're losing yourself. You're losing us, Lo."

I knew how hard this was for him. Seeing the pain in his eyes, and knowing I had caused it cut me to the core. Desperate to convince him this would be over soon, I pleaded with him to understand as tears spilled down my face.

"You're right, I've been drinking too much. I promise I'll slow down, and I plan to work less, too. But please, right now I need you to believe that we're not losing anything. I'll figure this out and find a way to keep The Grandview, and put us back together. You'll see.

"Keep The Grandview? What's going on, Lo?"

"Yes." I took a deep breath. This is not how I wanted to tell him. "Barry called today. Evelyn wants to sell her share, and I have ninety days to come up with the money to buy her out." I hesitated and buried my face in my hands as

I forced the words to come out, "Three hundred thousand dollars."

Jake leaned forward and hung his head. "Now what, Lo? You're going to make yourself crazy for the next three months trying to come up with the money? This is exactly what I'm talking about. We both know three months isn't long enough to come up with that kind of money. We don't have the resources for a loan and there isn't an investor in his right mind who would take a chance in this economy. Not that you would consider it anyway. It's impossible."

I felt my cheeks burning red. I could barely sit still. "Don't say that, Jake! Don't ever say that! Losing this place is not an option. This is my life!"

He shot back through gritted teeth, "What about losing me? Is losing me an option?"

His words sliced through me like a knife. "I need you Jake, please understand. I can make this work. Just let me get through these next few months and everything can get back on track. Back to the way we'd always planned."

"Lo, this is all too much. The only way I see out of this is to sell The Grandview. You could split the money with Evelyn and have something left for our future. We don't need some huge wedding like we planned. It just feels wrong now anyway. Let's just elope, put The Grandview on the market and elope. We could even move away if you want. I know you couldn't live here knowing someone else owned this place, and I've been meaning to tell you this, but the timing never seemed right," he paused and squeezed his hands together. "I was offered a job in Tennessee. It comes with a huge pay raise, big enough that you could take some time off to decide what you want your new career to be. What do you think? Will you go with me?"

I wanted to throw up, just lean forward and throw up all over the floor. I held my head between my hands trying to find my voice to answer. *Jake decided to take a job in Tennessee without even talking to me?*

"This is all too crazy. This impossible deadline. If I had the money you know I'd give it to you. I know how much this place means to you, but Lo, you've got to face it. This will break you if you let it."

My emotions shifted quickly. "No, Jake, losing this place would break me!"

"What happens in September when you can't meet the deadline? What then?"

Anger shook my entire body, and my words spewed out like venom. "Of all the people in my life I thought you would understand! This place is part of me, Jake. It's part of who I am! I've never imagined my life without it. I don't even know what to say. How could you ever expect…"

My tears were drowning me. I wasn't sure what I was saying, but I could hear the words coming out before the thoughts fully registered in my mind. My rock, my friend, the one thing solid left in my life was asking me to do the impossible, and the only thing worse is knowing that I deserved it. I betrayed his trust and took him for granted, and now here we were on the brink of disaster.

"We need to move on, Lo. I just want to put this all behind us before it's too late."

"Too late for what?" I tried to look at him through the tears flooding my eyes, but I couldn't read his face. I didn't know where he was going with this. Panic washed over me.

"Too late for you. Too late for us to have the life we deserve together before this place takes all that's left of you."

"Please, Jake, just stop this," I choked on the words.

"Lauren, I don't think you understand. I can't sit back and watch this consume you. I'm putting an end to it now. You need to make the rational decision here and cut your losses. We'll start over fresh in Tennessee. You need to stop and think about how good this could be for us. The way I see it, there's really no choice here."

"Are you asking me to choose?" *Now I understand what you're saying, you son-of-a-bitch! You want me to choose between you and the only thread that remains between me and my parents. You're threatening to abandon me when I need you the most. Fuck you, Jake Kennedy! Go ahead, tell me you're asking me to choose!*

Like a cornered animal, I let my fear consume me. Then rage. Looking him straight in the eye, I ripped the diamond from my finger and flung it in his lap. I chose. "Leave Jake Kennedy! Leave me like my mother and father did! Take your love and your promises, and leave just like they did. Like everything that's ever mattered in my life! That's what people do! They say they love you, and in the end they just leave! But you know what? You know what will always be with me, Jake? The Grandview that's what!

I'll never be alone as long as I have her, and I won't let anything stand in my way of keeping it that way!"

He looked away, and his body went rigid with anger as he caught the ring in mid-air and stood up without saying a word. When he walked out, I heard him lift his keys from the table where he left them ten minutes ago. Ten minutes ago--when I was still foolish enough to believe that I could hold on to the few precious things I had left.

I woke abruptly to the sound of a knock on my door. What time was it? I must have cried myself to sleep. I looked at the clock. 8:00 PM. I dragged the covers up higher not wanting to move, but the knocking continued until I reluctantly swung my legs over the side of the bed to find my flip-flops and shuffled to the door. Cracking it open I was met with the twisted worried expression on Nina's face.

"Lo, are you okay? Why haven't you called me?"

"Nice to see you, too" I retorted as I headed to the cupboard to find the bottle of vodka I was draining before deciding to crawl into bed and never get up.

"I'm heading home. The meeting is on for 8:30 tomorrow morning, and I've heard a few good ideas already."

"Sounds fabulous, Nina" I said without bothering to turn around.

"Seriously, Lo. What's going on now? I saw Jake's truck peel out of here like a bat out of hell a couple hours ago. Did you tell him about Evelyn?"

"Let's see, where to start? Well, how about if I start with the fact that I have no family left, my stepmother made away with my inheritance, and if that wasn't enough, now she's trying to take the family business away? The Grandview's future depends on me, and in case you haven't noticed I'm a real dependable, fucking girl these days! Oh, and let's not forget that the wedding is definitely off!"

"What? What do you mean the wedding is off? Lo, have you been drinking again?"

Yep, you got to love Nina. She let me ramble on unchallenged, and the only thing she heard was "the wedding is off!" Then she actually had the nerve to ask if *I* was drinking?

"No, Nina. I haven't had a drop in a few hours, but as a matter-of-fact, I am heading down to the bar right now. Let me buy you a drink, and I'll tell you all about it."

I expected her to decline after my sarcastic outburst, but she was always a true friend and loved me whether I was good, bad or ugly, so five minutes later we were sitting on barstools in the tavern. We ordered two Grey Goose martinis, and I began pouring my heart out to my best friend drink by drink by wonderful mind-numbing drink.

Everything that happened up until now seemed like a blur, but after saying it out loud to Nina it seemed more like reality. Jake was gone. He forced me to choose between him and The Grandview, and now he was gone.

I told Nina what he said, his exact words, his tone of voice, his body language, and she helped me analyze each detail like only a best friend could. I also told her about the money my dad had left me, and confessed every sordid detail about my weekend with Parker. I was careful to leave out the other conversation that transpired in Barry's office…although I'm not sure why. I was outraged at the time, but now… *Was I actually considering it?*

"What time is it getting to be?" Nina's voice broke through my thoughts.

"It's midnight," Steve said from behind the bar. "I was thinking about wrapping this up for the night ladies. Unless of course you would like another?"

I saw Nina yawning and knew she was ready to go. "Thanks Steve. I think we're all set, but I'll take one to go."

"Sure thing, Lo. Coming right up. Oh and, Nina, if you want I can give you a ride. It's right on my way."

Nina blushed. Even a fool could see it. Even a fool who'd just downed five martinis. "Is it serious?" I whispered in her ear.

"I hope so," she beamed. "I'm sorry. I didn't want to tell you I was happy when you're so…" She didn't have to finish.

"Nina," I stopped her, "I love you. I'm just glad to know there's one fucking ounce of happiness left in this world, and if anyone deserves it, it's you."

The flicker from the candles on the bar reflected in her teary eyes. "I love you, too, Lo. Do you want us to help you upstairs?"

"No, thanks, I'll be fine." I no sooner uttered the words when I felt the whole room start to tilt. "Um, yeah, maybe that would be a good idea."

I don't remember the walk to my suite, but at one point I felt a cool breeze on my face and heard the waves breaking on the beach. I remember thinking I wanted them to deposit me in a lounge chair on my balcony. The sounds soothed me. But before I knew it I was lying in bed, and Nina was removing my shoes.

"Don't forget the staff meeting at 8:30. I'll set your alarm for you."

She's setting an alarm for me. Thank you, Nina. When the door closed I started to wiggle out of my clothes piece by piece. I rolled over on my side and could almost feel the moonlight from the window floating over my body. A clean breeze tickled across my back and swirled around the undersides of my breasts.

Within seconds I was imagining Parker's hands on my body. *What's wrong with me?* Wetness pooled between my legs as flashbacks of our raw lovemaking went off in my mind like scenes from a home movie. *Didn't I love Jake at all?*

Maybe the gravity of what happened hadn't hit me yet. It wasn't safe to love him anymore. I needed to put the entire idea of *love* to rest. By now I was good at picking up the pieces after losing someone, and I knew I could take care of myself. Love was something that wasn't worth the risk, and I vowed that I wouldn't set myself up for the fall. I wouldn't let anyone that close again.

Thirteen

THE DEVIL'S IN THE DETAILS

As soon as the alarm blared my eyes opened, and I knew what I needed to do. I picked up the phone and dialed.

"Good morning, Lauren. I was hoping you would call." I could hear Barry's million dollar smile through the receiver.

"When do I leave?" A charge of anxiety surged through me as the words left my mouth. I didn't sound like myself. Butterflies gathered in my stomach, and I immediately began second guessing my decision.

"This afternoon. I don't want to give you time to change your mind. Mr. Blackwell will send his jet, and I'll call you with the details within the hour."

The image of being delivered in Parker's private jet like a shipment of expensive cargo he purchased rubbed me the wrong way. "No. I have one condition. I want a roundtrip ticket on a commercial airline. I'm agreeing to be a paid prostitute not a hostage."

"Lauren, you're really taking this out of context. It's more about companionship than sex."

"Save the bullshit, Barry. This is non-negotiable," I hissed.

"Very well, have it your way. In that case I'll pick you up at 9:30 and drive you to the airport myself, and remember no one can know about this Lauren."

"Then what do you suggest I tell them?"

"Tell them you're doing a consulting job for a friend of mine outside of Vegas. Your staff knows you need money, right? You'll be out of town this week for five days returning on Tuesday of next week. Oh, and pack light. Got it?"

"Yeah, sure."

"I'm not sure how well you know Mr. Blackwell, but he's one of my best clients, Lauren. He's a complete gentleman, so you'll have nothing to worry about."

"I doubt he's much of a gentleman, Barry, but then I'll be the judge of that. See you at 9:30."

Barry was laughing as I hung up the phone. *What am I doing? Selling your soul to the devil, Lo, that's what you're doing.* Unfortunately, it was my only option, the only way I could save what was left of my life. The thought sobered me. This was my one shot. I had to shut down any feelings I had left. Feelings were an overrated luxury I could no longer afford. The clock was ticking, and I needed to do whatever it took to make three hundred thousand dollars before my time was up. After the conversation with Jake last night it was clear that going to Vegas was my only option. I was angry, but deep inside I couldn't deny my curiosity. I was going to see Parker Blackwell's world first hand. I was exhilarated, and at the same time it scared me to death.

Funny how just when you think you have it all figured out, life throws you a curve ball. Only days ago, even hours ago, I was going to marry Jake, run The Grand and live happily ever after. Maybe things weren't perfect, but I stopped expecting perfection the day my mom died. Life was stable and that's all I could ask for. *How could Jake expect me to leave? How could he expect me to give up everything that mattered in my life without a fight?* I wondered if he ever really knew me at all, if he ever really loved me. Bitterness filled my chest. Determined I wouldn't let myself fall apart, I desperately searched for something good that I could cling to, and somehow I already knew what it would be. The idea itself was dangerous, and I knew I should leave it alone, but I needed something, anything to get me through this. I had to let down my guard and admit it.

Maybe it was just an illusion I chose to create, but seeing Parker after all these years brought me back to a place I had long forgotten. The moment his eyes searched mine, the moment our bodies connected for the first time, I became the girl I was before my world was shattered, and for a moment I felt unbroken, alive. Against all logical thought and ignoring my inner voice's warning, I threw caution to the wind and fell into his arms.

I knew we were two different people now, but when I was with him I felt like nothing had changed. Our connection was so strong it drew me to him. It fulfilled some dark need that only being with him could satisfy. But

I had to be careful. I had to keep my heart in a safe place. Parker was a player, a man who could have any woman he desired at any time, and by the sounds of it he never let his desires go unfulfilled. I tried to recall what he said about love and sex. I didn't remember his exact words, but it was something about there being a difference. I wondered why he chose to separate the two. *Was casual sex his defense against falling in love?*

I needed to stop trying to figure out what made Parker Blackwell tick. The truth is I may never know, and I didn't have the time or energy to waste worrying about it. The only thing I could be sure of was no matter what I had to do I was going to save The Grand. This was a business transaction and nothing more, and my contract said I just had to get through the next five days. How tough could it really be? I already had sex with the man, but the word "sex" didn't come close to describing what he did to me, the way. He claimed every part of me, his body sending signals mine just couldn't resist. *Pheromones!* I'd never felt so desired, and it was exhilarating beyond anything I'd ever experienced.

Yes, in my mind I was livid that he resorted to extortion, blackmail even, but my body was begging for more, and in the end we would both get exactly what we wanted. He purchased me to be his high priced call girl, and for the next five days I intended to give him exactly what he bargained for. I'll swallow my pride and play the role he was paying me to play. It would be worth it in the end when I left with his money and never looked back...at least that's what I told myself.

By the time I was dressed and ready for the meeting my mind felt clear. I was confident I was making the right decision. Before walking out the door, I instinctively checked my cell phone to see if Jake had called. *Stop it, Lo. There's no going back now only forward.*

I took the porch around to the large dining room. It took longer, but I wanted to feel the sunshine and breathe the fresh air as long as I could before I had to deliver an award winning performance to my staff. On the way, I rehearsed my lines one last time. *Don't say too much. Keep it brief. You might get caught up in the details if you're not careful.*

As I approached the conference room I could hear voices behind the door. I opened it, looked around and smiled at everyone confidently. My palms were wet, and I tried to keep my hands steady, but seeing their faces only confirmed that I was making the right choice. I couldn't let them down. My staff was top notch, and their families depended on the paychecks I signed. I stood behind my seat at the head of the table and leaned in close to whisper into Nina's ear,

"The box of money from my dad is in the safe. Take it to the bank, and make sure payroll gets out on time while

I'm gone. Don't worry. I'll call you soon." I gave her a little hug and a reassuring smile before addressing the staff, but she just blinked at me and looked confused.

"Good morning everyone. I have some news I need to share, but first I want to thank each and every one of you for stepping up to the plate to keep things running smoothly these past few months. It's because of you that we're the best on Lake Michigan, and we'll continue to welcome our guests back year after year," I pushed through the lump in my throat and continued, "I called you here this morning to personally ease your fears and erase any doubt you may have about the future of The Grandview. First, I want to announce that I'll be buying Evelyn's shares sometime within the next three months. It's not going to be easy. I'm going to have to take on some extra work to make it happen, but I know you'll keep this place running like a well-oiled machine while I'm gone, and things will get back to normal in no time. I have a plane to catch, so I'm going to turn the meeting over to Nina."

Nina's eyes opened wide when she heard her name. She shot me a concerned look, but then quickly recovered and pushed back from the table to stand next to me.

"I'm leaving this morning for Vegas. Mr. Stanton *ugh* has found me a job as a consultant to a small resort owned by a friend of his. I'll be home on Tuesday, but while I'm gone please see Nina if you have any issues. Thanks again, everyone. Things can only get better from here."

Standing up straight, my shoulders squared, I forced my best smile, making eye contact with each person at the table before turning and leaving the room. I'd made it through the meeting without falling apart, and my bag was packed. I was one step closer to fixing this damn mess and getting back home.

Barry pulled up in his Lexus right on time. As I wheeled my suitcase through the door he climbed out to give me a hand, and I did my best to hide my contempt as I watched him stow my suitcase neatly in back. *What a gentleman! Wonder if your wife knows about your little business in Vegas?*

He pulled his Ray-Ban sunglasses down to inspect me. "Lauren, you look radiant!" he beamed.

"Mmm hmm," I managed with a fake smile.

When he climbed in the car he handed me my ticket and a clipboard. "Your flight leaves at 12:30. You'll be flying out of Traverse City to O'Hare then connecting non-stop from there to Las Vegas. When you arrive my assistant will pick you up, and then Mr. Blackwell has arranged for a special surprise. Oh, and I need you to sign that paper," he threw in casually.

I raised my eyebrows suspiciously and examined his face. "Special surprise? What kind of surprise? And what exactly am I signing, Barry?"

"You'll see. Something to help you relax, maybe take the edge off a bit. Mr. Blackwell is a very important client of mine, Lauren. We need to make sure he's happy -- very happy. And the paper is a non-disclosure agreement. It basically says that you agree to keep this arrangement and anything that may happen during your stay confidential. Do you understand?"

So even hookers signed contracts these days? I scribbled my name quickly and shoved the clipboard at him asking him to elaborate in my most business-like tone. "What exactly does *very happy* mean, Barry? I thought you said sex wasn't required?" I wanted him to say the words. I wanted him to say it.

He quickly avoided the question, but I noticed with satisfaction that his knuckles were turning white from squeezing the steering wheel. *That's right you bastard. I want to see you squirm.*

"I think you're aware he's a world class poker player, right? Have you seen him on TV? When he comes to Vegas I make sure he's in good company for a few days before his tournaments. Helps him relax."

I wanted him to shut up. The smug son-of-a-bitch thought he was doing me a favor by feeding me meaningless details about a man with whom I'd exchanged much more with than just sordid business deals.

I sat with my fists balled in my lap, and before I could think I snapped, "Barry, two days ago I had the man's cock in my mouth, so unless you can tell me about something more meaningful than his hooker fetish, please spare me the small talk."

Barry's jaw dropped open in shock, and I smiled inside. Smacking him in the face couldn't have gotten his attention more effectively. When he finally looked back at the road he had to jerk the wheel to keep us from going off the edge. Maybe I was a little too bold, but it served him right, and besides, if I'm going to be nothing more than a high priced hooker for the next few days I might as well try on the shoes.

There was an awkward silence in the air during the rest of the ride, and I looked out the passenger window to avoid any further conversation. When we reached the airport, I felt Barry's eyes on my ass as I exited the car without saying a word and made my way through the revolving door. *How had I never noticed what a pig he was before?* I boarded the flight and found my seat quickly. The whole idea of going to Vegas seemed so surreal until this moment, and I wondered whether Jake heard that I'd left by now. I wondered if he even cared. Since my cell phone had been silent all day, I had to assume he didn't. Honestly, it didn't matter considering what I was about to do, and there was no turning back now.

In a weird way, pretending to be somebody else in a faraway place seemed like a luxury. For a moment I could escape reality and forget that everything around me was falling apart. I could stop trying to be strong and let go of all that I couldn't control. These thoughts seemed to calm my nerves, and I felt a faint smile on my lips as I thought of Nina and silently wished they could clear my chakras, too. I leaned my head back and reminded myself that in five short days The Grand would be mine, and for now that's all that really mattered.

As the plane lifted higher, and the vast beauty of Lake Michigan came into view, I reclined my seat and watched my home and all the problems I was leaving behind slowly fade away.

About the Author

First of all, if you're here, you're awesome! Thank you for purchasing my book!

I'm passionate about reading and writing steamy romance stories! However, over the years I've done a little of everything from bank manager to real estate agent to waitress--sometimes even simultaneously! I use these life experiences plus some secret fantasies (wink) to create unique material. WARNING-the content is scorching hot and full of surprises!

Today, I own an amazing business with my sister and bestie! We laugh, we cry, we cuss, but at the end of the day we share the same goals and dreams. Growing up we always wished we had been born into a family business. Since that wasn't the case we decided to start our own. It's been a crazy ride so far.

Even so, my obsession with starting new projects and "re-inventing myself" in general has driven me to publish my first novel. Eek! I've found there is nothing more exciting than creating my own little world on a page. So far I'm addicted! My nights consist of a bottomless coffee cup, a few Candy Crush Saga breaks and some loving nuzzles from my two dogs who are just thrilled with my new hours.

I'm anxious to see where this journey will lead, and for those of you who are with me...thank you from the bottom of my heart!

And with that I think Natasha Bedingfield said it best..."The rest is still UNWRITTEN!"

To connect with me please find me on:

Facebook

https://www.facebook.com/annicarossiauthor

Twitter

@AnnicaRossiAuth

OR on my website (Coming soon!)

https://www.annicarossi.com

www.ingramcontent.com/pod-product-compliance
Lightning Source LLC
Chambersburg PA
CBHW070813120626
46556CB00002B/479